Praise for Anne-Marie Conway's Butterfly Summer

"Secrets and mysteries abound in Anne-Marie Conway's haunting novel." *The Sunday Express*

"It could happily sit beside novels from the likes of Cathy Cassidy; what makes this one special is the brooding atmosphere of secrets waiting to be discovered, which builds like a gathering summer storm."
Books For Keeps

"A gripping story which catches the importance of friendship – even when there are dark, dark secrets." Love Reading 4 Kids

"She has a wonderful writing style which makes the book hard to put down." YA Yeah Yeah blog

"I adored this book... It was sad, gripping, touching, surprising, exciting and everything you could want from a great book." What Lexie Loves blog

About the author

Anne-Marie Conway is a primary school teacher specializing in drama, who also runs her own children's theatre company, Full Circle. She lives in London with her husband, two young sons and two eccentric cats, Betty and Boo.

She is an award-winning author of acclaimed mystery stories, including *Butterfly Summer*, which was selected for the Summer Reading Challenge 2012 and Bookbuzz 2013, and *Forbiddden Friends*, which won the Southwark Book Award 2014.

Find out more about Anne-Marie at
www.annemarieconway.com

Tangled Secrets

Anne-Marie Conway

USBORNE

For Paula:

the best big sister anyone could wish for.

First published in the UK in 2015 by Usborne Publishing Ltd., Usborne House, 83-85 Saffron Hill, London EC1N 8RT, England. www.usborne.com

Text copyright © Anne-Marie Conway, 2015

Cover photo © Markovka /Shutterstock

Title lettering by Stephen Raw. Chapter illustrations by Antonia Miller. Butterfly illustrations by Joyce Bee.

The name Usborne and the devices ♀ ⊕ are Trade Marks of Usborne Publishing Ltd.

A CIP catalogue record for this book is available from the British Library.

ISBN 9781409570332 J MAMJJASOND/15 03194/1

Printed in the UK.

Six Months Ago

I didn't understand what was happening at first. It was Sunday morning, three weeks before Christmas, and Nan and I were walking up to the shops, our arms linked together against the cold. We were going to make a crumble for pudding and we had all the ingredients we needed except for flour. Nan's crumble was the best, especially her apple and blueberry; it was all soft and sweet and gooey.

I was just telling her about my purple ribbon, how I was going to stop sleeping with it under my pillow – how babyish it was to have a comforter now I was in Year Eight

– how Mum kept nagging me to get rid of it. I was talking away non-stop, listing all the reasons I didn't need it any more, but I had a funny feeling Nan wasn't listening properly.

"Did you hear me, Nan?" I shook her arm to get her attention. "I've set myself a target. I'm *definitely* going to stop sleeping with my ribbon by the end of Year Eight. I could probably give it up right now if I really wanted to, it's just…"

I stopped for a second and glanced up at her. Something was wrong. She was breathing funny, leaning against me, but not in a cosy, cuddly way, more like she needed me to hold her up.

"Nan?" I tried to keep her steady, to stop her slipping, but she was too heavy. "Nan, what's the matter?"

She shuddered slightly and then let out a long, strangled groan, a horrible sound that I'd never heard before, slumping down onto the pavement.

"Nan! Nan! What's wrong?" I dropped to my knees next to her. "What's wrong? Get up, Nan! Please, get up, you're scaring me! I don't know what to do!"

She was gasping for breath, trying to say something, but her words were thick and slurred, impossible to understand.

I looked around, my heart thumping wildly. I needed

an ambulance. I had to call for an ambulance. I pulled my phone out of my pocket, but I couldn't make my fingers work properly, they wouldn't press the right numbers, they were too big and clumsy and the screen was blurred.

"Help!" I cried, but it came out as a whisper. "Please. My nan's ill! Please, someone, help me."

A man ran across from the other side of the road. "Something's wrong with my nan," I tried to say, but nothing came out. "We were going to the shops. We were going to make a crumble. I was just telling her…I was just…" My mouth was moving but I couldn't hear anything, it was like someone had switched the sound off.

The man seemed to know what to do. He put his coat over Nan to keep her warm and called for an ambulance. He held her hand and talked to her, telling her over and over that everything was going to be okay. He asked me my name and if I knew my mum's phone number. I think I told him, or tried to at least, but I can't remember. I can't remember anything very clearly after that, except for Nan's twisted-up face, and the horrible choking noises she was making, and how desperately I needed my purple ribbon.

Missing Nan

Nan had been dead for exactly six months on the day Sharon called. I had no idea there was any connection at the time, between Nan and Sharon – I only found that out much later.

It was a Monday afternoon in June, the first day back after half-term, and I was home alone, sitting at the kitchen table doing my homework. I didn't bother answering the phone at first – I was in the middle of a tricky comprehension and I knew it wouldn't be for me – but a moment later it rang again, and then again.

My heart began to beat a bit too fast. Why would someone call so many times? Why didn't they just leave a message on the machine? I started to imagine the worst: the police calling to say Mum or Dad had been in an accident, or after-school club calling to say Charlie was hurt. I told myself not to be stupid, but when it rang again I snatched it up, my hand damp with sweat.

"Hello?"

"Can I speak to Oliver Wilkins, please?"

It was a woman asking for Dad, but I didn't recognize her voice.

"He's not in at the moment," I said, wishing I'd left it to ring. "Can I take a message?"

There was a long silence.

"Hello? Can I take a message?"

"Sorry, yes, I'm still here," said the woman. "Could you write down this number and ask him to call me as soon as he gets in?"

I reached for the notepad where we write phone messages and she read out a mobile number, and then repeated it really slowly.

"Who shall I say it is?" I asked when she'd finished.

I could hear her breathing but she didn't say anything.

"Hello? Who is it?"

"Sorry," she said, her voice catching slightly. "It's Sharon. Just tell him it's Sharon."

There were a few more ragged breaths then a click and then nothing.

She'd rung off without saying goodbye.

I couldn't concentrate on my comprehension after that. I spent ages doodling my name across the top of the page in bubble writing and then shaded in the letters using different colours. I've been finding it harder and harder to concentrate lately. I have these stupid thoughts that go round and round my head like a toy car on a track.

Sometimes I can make them go away – if I'm watching something good on telly or sketching in my art book – but it doesn't take long for them to creep back in, especially when I'm at school. It usually starts with a question, like, *why did my nan have to die?* And then that leads to another question, and then another, until whole chunks of the lesson have disappeared while I try to work out the answers.

I glanced up at the kitchen clock, willing the hands to move faster, wishing Mum and Charlie would hurry up. Nan used to pick Charlie up from school when Mum was working. She'd bring him back here and make our tea while I sat at the table, doing my homework, nattering on about my day.

The house was too quiet now. It felt too empty. Charlie

goes to the after-school care club and I have a key to let myself in. I'm usually only home alone for an hour, max, but it seems to stretch on and on. The first thing I do is turn on the radio, and sometimes the TV as well, to help drown out the silence.

I'd just about finished shading the last letter of my name using my favourite colour, dark purple, when I heard Charlie bursting through the front door like a mini-torpedo.

"We're home, Maddie!" he yelled from the hall. "And you'll never believe what's happened!"

He came crashing into the kitchen, knees bent in one way, feet sticking out the other, fists clenched by his sides. "I *still* didn't get picked for the football team. It's so unfair. Mr Maddox handed out the letters at the end of the day and Rory and Leo got picked but I'm not even a sub!"

Charlie was born nearly three months early – imagine a bag of sugar and that's how tiny he was. The doctors didn't even think he'd survive the first night. He's nine now, and more or less fine, except he's still pretty small for his age and his legs are sort of twisted in the middle and very skinny.

"Hey, what does Mr Maddox know?" I started to say – I hated seeing him upset – but he was already off, racing into the garden to kick a ball against the wall. Mum staggered in behind him carrying a load of shopping bags.

"Turn the radio down, Mads, for goodness' sake, we could hear it halfway down the road. I honestly don't know why you have to have it on so loud."

A few minutes later every surface in the kitchen was covered in packets and boxes and bags. I got up to help, pleased for an excuse to stop doing my homework – or *pretending* to do it anyway.

"Listen to this," said Mum, waving a bag of pears at me. "According to a report I was reading at lunchtime, pears are the new superfood. They've actually got more fibre in them than a whole box of bran flakes."

She tipped the pears into a bowl, grabbing one and holding it up to the light as if she might actually *see* the fibre. She comes up with a different "superfood" every few weeks. It was blueberries last time and fresh ginger the time before that. It's all part of her mission to Help Charlie Grow. He's got his annual check-up in a few weeks and she'll be gutted if he hasn't shot up at least a few centimetres – not that she'd ever let on to Charlie.

When we'd finished unpacking and everything was in its proper place, she made herself a cup of tea and sat down at the table.

"I do feel sorry for Charlie," she said, glancing out of the window. "I wish they'd give him a go in the football team, even for one game. I know he's not as strong as the others but it would give him such a boost. How about you, Mads? How was school?"

"Okay," I said.

"Did you get your mid-term assessments back?"

I shook my head, my face growing hot. "I think we're getting them tomorrow...Mrs Palmer had all this other stuff to hand out and she ran out of time."

We always do loads of tests at the end of each half-term and then find out the results first day back. I hated lying to Mum but there was no way I was telling her what I actually got. All my grades were down except for art, and my effort marks were rubbish. I was supposed to be seeing Mrs Palmer tomorrow to have a *little chat about my progress*, but there was no way I was telling Mum about that either.

I picked up my pen, trying to dodge her gaze. I had no idea if she believed me or not – she was probably too worried about Charlie and the football team to notice anyway.

"I've got to finish my homework," I said. "It's taking ages. Oh and someone called for Dad." I pushed the notepad across the table.

Mum glanced down at it, frowning. "*Sharon?*"

I nodded, watching her face. "Do you know her?"

She picked the notepad up still staring at the number. "No I don't think so. What did she say?"

"Nothing really. She just left this number and asked if Dad would call her."

We'd finished eating dinner and cleared away by the time Dad came home from work. He's an electrician so he often finishes late. As soon as I heard his key in the door I started to relax. No reason really, just the fact that everyone was home. It's been like that ever since Nan died – a niggling worry that Mum or Dad or Charlie might be snatched away from me at any moment.

Charlie rushed out to greet Dad, launching into the whole football saga before he'd even said hello. We used to fight to tell him our news when he got in from work, tripping over each other to get to the front door, but not any more. I could easily get there first if I wanted, I'm much faster than him – it's getting the actual words out that I find so difficult.

I hovered by the door, listening to Charlie babbling away. People always used to say we were identical, me and Charlie – two little chatterboxes with the same shiny dark hair, pale skin and turquoise-blue eyes. We still look the same, obviously, but there's only one chatterbox in the house these days.

Dad scooped Charlie up for a hug and carried him back in to the kitchen, laughing. "What a welcome!" he said. "You nearly knocked me clean off my feet! And how are my two favourite girls?" He plonked Charlie down and opened the fridge to pull out a beer. "I can't get over this weather! It's only the first week of June and it's already nudging twenty-seven degrees."

"I've left some pasta for you on the stove, if you're hungry," said Mum. "And someone called Sharon rang – she wants you to call her back."

"Sharon?" He paused to take a swig of his drink. "I don't know anyone called Sharon. It was probably one of those cold-callers trying to sell me something."

I was pretty sure it *wasn't* someone trying to sell him something. The woman sounded really upset. I opened my mouth to tell him so and then shut it again. If it was that important she could always call back.

Dad heaped the rest of the pasta into a bowl and collapsed on the couch to watch the football with Charlie. It was England against Holland and England were losing 3–0. I sat down next to him, tucking my legs up and snuggling in. "Can you believe this, Maddie?" he said, pointing at the screen, but I wasn't really interested in the game – I just wanted a cuddle.

A few days after Nan died I looked up strokes online to see if they run in families. I found out that if you have a parent who had a stroke before the age of sixty-five you're four times more likely to have a stroke yourself. I didn't understand the statistics or how they worked it all out, but since Nan was Dad's mum *and* she was only sixty-three when she died, it sounded as if Dad could drop dead at any moment.

Charlie was still going on about the school team when Mum took him up to bed at half-time. He said he was determined to get picked before the end of the year – to prove he was as good as Rory and Leo if it was the last thing he did.

"That's the spirit," said Dad. "The England team could do with some of your skills right now judging by this pathetic performance!"

When Mum came back down she made herself another cup of tea and started the ironing, pulling one of her work shirts out of a mountain of wrinkly clothes.

"Hey, Sophie," said Dad, dragging his eyes away from the screen. "Did you hear the one about the woman who went to visit her elderly dad in the old-age home? She walked into his room and said, 'For goodness' sake, isn't there anyone here who could iron your clothes?' And the old man looked at his daughter and said, 'What are you talking about? I'm not *wearing* any clothes!'"

Dad started to laugh and I couldn't help laughing with him. "Do you get it?" he said to Mum. "The man wasn't actually *wearing* any clothes. It was his *skin*! His skin was so wrinkled she thought it needed an iron. Who needs ironed clothes anyway?" he added, still laughing. "Life's too short if you ask me."

"Actually no one did ask you," said Mum, rolling her eyes, but I could tell she was trying not to laugh too. And for a tiny moment, with Mum ironing her shirt and Dad cracking jokes and messing about, I could almost pretend that everything was just the way it used to be.

I had the dream again that night. The one where Nan and I are walking along the road together and I'm talking to her, but my words are all strung together like one long sentence – hundreds and hundreds of words pouring out of my mouth like an avalanche. And when I turn to see if she's listening I realize she's lying on the pavement, completely still, as if she's made of stone. "*Wake up, Nan!*" I shout. "*Wake up! Wake up! Wake up!*" But it's at that point that I wake up myself, my heart racing, my face wet with tears.

I've been having the same dream on and off ever since Nan died. The details change a bit each time, but it always ends the same way. I *hate* the dream. I don't want to remember Nan like that – cold and frozen and still. My nan was soft and warm, like apple and blueberry crumble, full of stories and jokes and the cleverest wise words.

It took me ages to fall back to sleep, for the images to fade completely from my head. I reached under my pillow for my purple ribbon, curling it round my fingers, rubbing it against my face. The knots in my stomach unravelled slowly and I snuggled down under my covers.

Nan used to say I shouldn't be embarrassed about sleeping with my ribbon – she said it was just like a teddy, or a comfort blanket – but who needs a comfort blanket when they're nearly thirteen years old?

2

The Nurture Group

It was a struggle to get out of bed the next morning. I wondered if I could pretend to be ill to get out of my meeting with Mrs Palmer, except I knew Mum would never go for it, not unless I actually threw up or had a raging temperature. Charlie only has to cough for Mum to keep him at home but it's a whole different story with me.

I dragged myself up and out of the house on automatic pilot. It usually takes me about twenty minutes to walk to school, but much longer when I go extra slow on purpose. I slowed down even more when I got to the corner of Banner Road, just in case the new boy Kieran Black was there. He's been on my case ever since he joined Church

Vale in January, winding me up, calling me stupid names like "Maddie Mouse".

I kept my head down as I came up Banner Road, relieved there was no sign of him – praying he'd get sick of picking on me if I managed to stay out of his way. Gemma was waiting for me just outside the main gates looking as neat and tidy as usual, her thick brown hair tied into two perfect plaits.

"Hurry up, Maddie!" she called out, running to meet me. "Did you finish your comprehension? It took me hours and hours to do mine and it was *soooo* boring. I nearly gave up to be honest, but seriously, you know what Miss Owen's like…"

She chatted non-stop all the way into school, flicking her plaits over her shoulders as we made our way down the corridor towards our lockers. Gemma and I have been best friends for ever. We were paired up in our very first lesson at Church Vale and we've been pretty much inseparable ever since – the sort of friends who share everything.

If I had to describe Gemma in three words I'd say she's clever, clever and clever! She's easily the cleverest girl in Year Eight. Some of the others think she's a swot, especially in maths and science – always getting the best grades, always the first to hand in her homework – but they're just jealous. It's not as if she ever shows off about it.

She was brilliant when I first told her about Nan; she actually cried on the phone when I explained what had happened. I was off school for ages – two weeks before Christmas plus an extra two weeks for the holidays – but she rang me nearly every day to see how I was feeling and to fill me in on all the gossip. She said she couldn't wait for me to come back, but that I was lucky I'd missed my end-of-term assessments, especially one of Madame Dupont's killer French tests.

It really helped to talk to her, and even to laugh about the test, but for some weird reason, once I was back at school, neither of us mentioned Nan again, almost as if it never happened. We went straight back to talking about rotational symmetry and history projects and how much we both hate Kieran Black – and I have no idea how to tell her that I don't really care about any of that stuff any more, that I'm not even listening half the time.

I might seem okay on the outside, but on the inside I'm still struggling to understand how everything can change from one split second to the next.

There were the usual announcements at registration: one of the boys' toilets was blocked up; the guitar teacher was ill so there wouldn't be any lessons. I wasn't paying much attention to be honest, but then, just before the bell, Mrs Palmer called my name and asked me to stay behind for a few moments.

"It's nothing to worry about, Maddie," she said, as the others filed out. "I just wanted to remind you that we're meeting today at lunchtime…"

She paused for a moment as if she expected me to say something. *Anything.* I practised the words in my head – *Okay, Mrs Palmer. Don't worry, I won't be late.* It should've been so easy, but *thinking* the words wasn't the same as actually *saying* them. I opened my mouth and closed it again, my face growing hot. It's been like this ever since Nan died. A panicky feeling whenever people are waiting for me to speak, like the words are stuck in my throat and something bad might happen if I dare to let them out.

"In my office at twelve then," she said eventually, a sorry look in her eyes. "It won't take long."

I hate it when she looks at me like that, like I'm a massive let down. She used to say I was one of her best students, an asset to the class. At the end of my first half-term in Year Eight she described me as *a happy, chatty, likeable girl who always tries her best.* I stared over her shoulder wishing I could turn the clock back, wishing I could make her proud of me again…

22

There was a sign on the wall with one of those motivational quotes.

Talking about your goals is the first step towards achieving them.

I was talking about my "goals" when Nan collapsed. Going on and on about my ribbon and how I was going to give it up. I remember how happy I felt as we walked into town that day, chatting away without a care in the world, looking forward to Christmas, and then – BAM!

"Maddie? *Maddie!* I said it won't take very long… Maddie? Are you okay?"

I dragged my eyes away from the sign and back to Mrs Palmer's face, forcing myself to focus on what she was saying; nodding to show her I was fine, that I was listening.

"I'll see you at lunchtime," she said slowly. "Off you go or you'll be late for class."

Gemma had saved me a place. She leaned over to ask me what was going on but Miss Owen shot her a warning look and held a finger up to her lips. No one messes about in Miss Owen's lessons, apart from Kieran Black; they wouldn't dare. She's the sort of teacher who gives out detentions for breathing.

We've been doing autobiographical accounts this term – researching famous autobiographies like Nelson

Mandela's *A Long Walk to Freedom*. It was a really good topic to start off with, especially the Nelson Mandela bit, but now we're supposed to be writing our own autobiographies – or, as Miss Owen put it, *a lively and interesting account of our lives so far including important events and significant milestones.*

I'd written loads about Charlie being born. How he had to spend the first three months of his life in the special baby unit. How many times he stopped breathing. How he was too small to fit into any of the normal-sized baby clothes or normal-sized nappies. How Mum had to use a special machine to breastfeed him. How she and Dad were up at the hospital so much Nan had to move in to look after me.

It was Nan who settled me in to Banner Road Nursery, the *second* significant milestone in my life. Charlie was home by then but he still needed lots of extra care. Nan said I screamed the place down on the first day, clinging onto her like a limpet – and that I carried on like that for weeks and weeks. She said the first time I ran into the classroom without a backwards glance she stood in the middle of the playground with the other mums and cheered.

I started to doodle the word LIMPET across the top of the page. I tried to make the letters cling onto each other like a real limpet clings onto a rock, adding little shells and starfish as I went along, shading the starfish using this special technique we've been learning in art to make them look more three-dimensional and lifelike.

I'd almost got all the way across the page when Gemma nudged me. I glanced up and realized Miss Owen was standing right in front of me with her arms folded, tapping her foot.

"Maddie Wilkins, are you with us, or do I have to send out a search party?" she said, not even trying to hide her sarcasm.

A few of the others began to laugh. She'd probably said my name at least four times by then. "I *said* I'd like you to read out the beginning of your autobiography, please."

I scraped my chair back and stood up, wiping my palms on my skirt, staring down at my book. My opening paragraph seemed very personal suddenly. I didn't want to tell everyone about Charlie being premature and there was no way I was going to say the word "breastfeed" in front of the entire class.

"Come on then, Maddie," said Miss Owen. "We don't need to hear the whole thing, just the first couple of sentences will do. Beginnings are so important."

I knew I was going to cry. I could feel the tears building up. Reading my work out in front of the others has become a total nightmare. I swallowed hard, trying to clear the lump in my throat, blinking very fast to stop the tears coming, but just at that moment Kieran Black yelled "DRUM ROLL!" and started to bang his hands on the table.

I closed my eyes waiting for him to stop but the banging got louder and louder. It got so loud I had to put my hands over my ears. Miss Owen swung round to face him. "Pack it in, Kieran!" she yelled over the noise but he just laughed at her and carried on banging as if he was playing the drums in a band.

He doesn't care what Miss Owen or any of the other teachers think of him – the only thing he cares about is winding me up, like he's made it his life's mission or something. I have no idea why, it's not as if I've ever done anything to him – maybe he's just desperate to get a reaction from Maddie Mouse, the quietest girl in Year Eight.

Miss Owen had to send him to the head, Mr Rawlins, in the end. She barked at us to carry on with our writing and followed him out to make sure he didn't disappear. As soon as she left the room I sank back down, relieved it was over, burying my face in my book.

"He's such a loser," said Gemma, trying to make me feel better. "I'd like to hear the beginning of *his* autobiography – his parents probably took one look at him and ran away screaming!"

* * *

I'd only ever been in Mrs Palmer's office once, back in September, when she met with us one at a time to talk about settling into Year Eight. It was just over eight months ago but it felt more like eight years. It was very neat and tidy, with alphabetical files on the shelves and framed photos of her family on the walls.

"Sit yourself down, Maddie," she said, pointing to the chair facing her desk. "It's much cooler in here, thank goodness. Can you feel the breeze?"

I nodded, and sat down quickly, tucking my skirt under my legs. Mrs Palmer sat opposite me, and opened a brand-new green folder with *Maddie Wilkins* written across the front. I stared at it nervously; it looked so official.

"I wanted to have a little chat about how things are going," she started. "I've seen your mid-term assessments, obviously, but it's not just your grades I'm concerned about. I've heard from other members of staff that you're finding it very difficult to speak in class, that you never put your hand up any more or join in with discussions…"

She was giving me the sorry look again. I stared down at the folder, wondering what was in it.

"You've always been one our best students," she went on. "Hard-working, confident, *chatty*. But if I'm honest, you seem to be struggling at the moment."

I wanted to say I was sorry, that I couldn't help it, but my mouth was too dry.

"I was just wondering if there was anything in particular bothering you, at home or at school? I know that you lost your nan recently, Maddie, and I do understand how hard it can be to concentrate on your work if you're feeling upset. How much it can get in the way..."

I raised my eyes to look at her again. Mum had phoned in to tell her about Nan when it happened back in December, when I was off school. But how was I supposed to explain that I was worried *all* the time – that I had a constant knot of anxiety in my tummy like I'd swallowed too many sour sweets in one go and they'd got all clogged up inside me.

"Now I can't force you to talk to me," said Mrs Palmer gently. "But we'd love to see the old Maddie back, the old *happy* Maddie..."

She paused for a moment, nodding and smiling, as if I could somehow pull the *old* Maddie out of a hat, right there and then in her office – as if it was as simple as that.

"So the thing is, Maddie," she went on when I didn't

28

say anything, "I've decided to put together a small Year Eight nurture group."

A *nurture group?* What on earth was a *nurture group?*

"I'll be calling your mum and dad later today, to talk to them about your progress in general and about the group, and to get their permission for you to attend, but a lady called Vivian is going to come to the school twice a week for the next six weeks, until we break up for the summer holidays. She's a trained counsellor and she'll be meeting with you and one or two others from Year Eight. It will be very relaxed and informal, so there's really nothing for you to worry about."

A *counsellor?* Did I really need to see a *counsellor?* And why did Mrs Palmer have to talk to Mum and Dad? They didn't even know about my assessments yet – they'd be upset enough about that. I could just imagine what Mum would say, how disappointed she would be.

"I know it might sound scary, the thought of talking to a stranger, but in my experience it's never a good idea to bottle things up." She opened the folder and started to write something down. "This will be the first time we've run a nurture group at Church Vale," she said, scribbling away, "but I've got a feeling it might be just what you need."

I sat very still, my whole body burning up, trying to work out what she was really saying. A *nurture group.*

What did it actually mean? Who else would be in it? Would everyone know? Vivian's *special* group. We'd be like the freaks of the class.

"Do I have to do it?" I whispered, forcing the words out, my heart hammering against my chest.

She paused for a moment, glancing up. "I would like you to give it a go, but *please* don't think of it as a punishment, and it's certainly nothing to be ashamed of. We all need a little bit of help sometimes, Maddie."

I stared down at my lap, willing my heart to slow down. Mrs Palmer was right, I did need help. But no one could undo the past or change what had happened, however well trained they were.

"The first meeting will be next Monday at nine. It means you'll miss registration, but we'll let you know if there are any important announcements. The meetings will take place in the Blue Room just along the corridor from the art supplies cupboard. Do you know where I mean?"

Of course I knew – *everyone knew*. The Blue Room was where all the "special needs" sessions were held.

I went to look for Gemma and found her having lunch in the canteen.

"What did Mrs Palmer want?" she asked, shifting up

to make room for me. "You're not in trouble are you?"

I shook my head, glancing round the canteen. I really wanted to tell her, but it was so embarrassing, like admitting out loud that there was something seriously wrong with me. Most of the Year Eights were sitting in big noisy groups, all trying to speak over each other. It was difficult to imagine they had a single worry between them.

I closed my eyes for a moment, wishing I had my purple ribbon with me. I'd do anything to be as happy and carefree as they seemed to be, to feel normal again, even for five minutes, but there was no way I could go to a *nurture group*.

How was I supposed to open up to a complete stranger when I couldn't even talk to my best friend?

3
The Woman in the Cemetery

Gemma wanted to hang out after school. A few of the others were going to the park to get ice creams from the cafe and she was desperate for us to tag along. She pressed her hands together under her chin, practically pleading with me to go, but I couldn't face it – pretending to have fun while Mrs Palmer was probably calling Mum right that minute to tell her about the nurture group and my grades and how badly I was doing.

"Come on, Maddie," she said when I shook my head. "We don't have to stay for long. Just for a bit, *please.*"

"I'm sorry, Gem, I can't. I've got way too much

homework, stuff I didn't do over half-term. I haven't even started my history project…"

"Why don't I come back to yours then? I've nearly finished mine but I really don't mind helping you…"

I shook my head again, searching for another excuse, but she turned to go before I could think of anything. Why was she so desperate to hang out at the park anyway? We used to spend all of our free time together, on our own.

"Suit yourself," she said, her voice flat. "I'm going anyway. I'll see you later."

She walked off in the direction of the park without looking back. I felt terrible. I should've just told her about the meeting with Mrs Palmer and the nurture group; it's not as if she'd laugh at me or anything. But then she'd want to know *why* I had to join and who else was in it and a million other details and I'd already decided I wasn't going, even if I had to beg Mum to write me a note or tell Mrs Palmer when she called.

I trailed home down Banner Road and through the cemetery, stopping to sit on my favourite bench. It's one of those really ancient cemeteries filled with old, faded gravestones and a huge weeping willow. It's nearly always empty during the week apart from maybe one or two people visiting a grave, or cutting through from Morley Avenue to Banner Road.

Mum was worried at first when she realized the route I took to and from school was straight through the cemetery. She thought it might upset me, walking past Nan's grave every day, but it's just the opposite. I like going there. I don't talk to her or anything; I just find it comforting to know she's still close by.

I remember asking Nan once if she believed in heaven. We were at the funfair on a ride that went so high you could almost touch the sky.

"Do you believe it's like a real place," I said, "with angels and harps and pearly gates?"

Nan opened her mouth to answer but just at that moment the ride plunged back down to earth and we clung hold of each other, eyes shut tight, screaming our heads off.

"I'll tell you what, Mads," she said later as we sat on the grass eating warm, sugary doughnuts, our hands sticky with jam. "I don't know about pearly gates and angels, but jammy doughnuts on a summer's day with my favourite granddaughter – that's my idea of heaven."

I'm not sure how long I'd been sitting on the bench when I noticed a woman coming through the old, rusty gate. She was about Mum's age, wearing jeans and trainers with a blue silk scarf wrapped tight around her head, covering her hair. I pulled my legs up under my chin and watched as she began to pick her way through the graves, stopping to read each one in turn.

Some people like to walk around the cemetery out of curiosity, to read the words that have been etched into the ancient stone for hundreds of years, but as the woman got closer I realized that she must be searching for a particular grave. She was clutching a small bunch of flowers in one hand and a wad of tissues in the other.

I decided to try and draw her in my sketchbook. I love, love, *love* drawing. I'd happily do it all day long if I had the choice. Drawing, sketching, doodling – anything really as long as it involves a piece of paper and a pencil. I reached into my bag for my book – I always have it with me just in case I see something interesting or pretty. When I looked up again I saw the woman had stopped right by Nan's grave.

She stood very still for a few moments and then kneeled down to arrange the flowers. Nan had loads of friends, the church was crammed full on the day of her funeral, but I was pretty sure I'd never seen this particular woman before. I watched as she traced her finger over the words engraved on the headstone: *In loving memory of Rosemary Wilkins – taken from us too soon. Forever missed by all who knew her.*

It felt strange sitting there, watching her. I wondered if

I should go over and introduce myself, ask her how she knew Nan, but I wasn't sure if I'd be able to get the words out. Maybe she knew my granddad too. He's buried in the grave right next to Nan's. He died a long time ago, years before I was born.

I was still trying to pluck up the courage to go over and talk to her when she stood up again and pulled something out of her pocket. I thought it was more tissues at first, but then I saw it was a crumpled piece of paper. She kneeled back down, smoothed it out and placed it on the grave, using a small stone to stop it from blowing away.

It was like something straight out of a movie. I was dying to know what it said. I held my breath as she stood there for another minute, dabbing at her eyes with the tissues, and then turned to go. She didn't look back once as she picked her way through the graves and out of the gate, disappearing down Morley Avenue.

My phone buzzed in my pocket, making me jump. It was a text from Mum asking where I was. It was obviously later than I realized, either that or she'd come home early. I texted back that I'd be five minutes and stuffed my sketchbook into my bag. Mrs Palmer must've called her and told her about my grades and the nurture group.

I trailed across the path and over to Nan's grave before I left. I wasn't in any hurry to get back, not if Mum was going to start having a go. Close up I could see the flowers were pink tulips, Nan's favourites. The woman had propped them up against the back of the headstone, the piece of paper placed just in front. The writing was small, the letters squashed together, and I had to kneel down to make it out.

My heart skipped a beat when I saw what it said.

I'm so sorry…forgive me x

I made my way out of the cemetery, my head in a spin. Who was she? And why was she saying sorry? I racked my brain trying to remember if I'd ever seen her before. She must've known Nan pretty well to know her favourite flowers were pink tulips. Perhaps they'd had a row before she died and never made up – although it was hard to imagine Nan falling out with anyone for very long. She always said life was too short to bear a grudge.

Mum was on the phone in the kitchen when I got in. I closed the front door as quietly as I could and crept upstairs before she could see me. As soon as I was in my room I pulled my ribbon out from under my pillow and wrapped it round my hand, holding it up to my face to breathe in the satiny smell.

I've had my purple ribbon under my pillow for as long

as I can remember – and not just my one special piece, there are old, tatty scraps squirrelled away all over the house for emergencies. I can't actually get to sleep without it. According to Nan it all started on my third birthday, just after Charlie was born. Mum and Dad were up at the hospital and Nan had moved in to look after me.

She said she tried to make the day as special as she could. She baked my favourite cake and decorated the house with loads of balloons, but I was so upset I didn't stop crying for Mum all afternoon. I didn't even cheer up when Nan gave me my present, a talking doll wrapped in purple paper with a purple satin ribbon.

Apparently I'd seen that doll in a shop and been desperate to have it. It was called My First Baby and if you pressed its tummy it said "I'm hungry", or "My nappy needs changing", or "I love you", in a proper baby voice. Nan thought I'd be thrilled, she said she couldn't wait to see my face, but as soon as the doll was out of the box I chucked it on the floor and cuddled up to her on the couch, the long, satin ribbon wrapped tight around my hand.

And then the following year, on my fourth birthday, when Charlie was home and everything was more settled, I still wanted all my presents wrapped in purple ribbon, and that's the way it's been ever since. I don't remember any of this of course; I only know there's something about having that first piece of ribbon tucked under my pillow, rubbing it against my face, breathing in the satiny smell, that makes me feel safe.

Mum didn't mention Mrs Palmer calling until just before bedtime when we were on our own. She sat on the edge of my bed, folding and refolding the edge of my sheet as if she was trying to work out what to say. In the end we both started speaking at the same time.

"I had a chat with Mrs Palmer this afternoon," she said, just as I said, "There was this woman in the cemetery…"

"I'm sorry, Mum," I cut in quickly before she got cross. "I was going to tell you about my mid-term assessments, I swear…"

"It's not really your grades I'm worried about, Mads," she said tightly, "although I was surprised. Mrs Palmer says you've been finding it difficult to concentrate – that you're teary and withdrawn. She says she used to have a job keeping you quiet, but that lately, apart from when you're with Gemma, you hardly say anything at all. She's concerned about you, Maddie, and so am I to be honest…" She paused for a moment, folding and refolding. "Look, I know you're missing Nan, that it's been a difficult time for you, but I didn't realize things had got as bad as this."

"As bad as what?" I said, although I knew exactly what she meant.

"I mean we're *all* missing Nan, Mads. It was a terrible shock for the whole family. But if only you'd *talk* to me. If only you'd tell me what's upsetting you *so* much instead of bottling it all up inside."

I could hear the impatience in her voice. I pulled my covers up and turned to face the wall, twisting my ribbon round my hand. I didn't know *how* to talk to Mum about Nan, or how it was supposed to help. I was used to talking to *Nan* about *Mum*, not the other way round.

"There was this woman in the cemetery," I tried again, my voice muffled through the sheets. "She was wearing a scarf around her head and…"

"Maddie, stop. We're not talking about that now. And I'm not sure you should even be hanging around the cemetery so much. It doesn't seem to be helping as far as I can see…"

"Helping what?" I said, my eyes filling with tears.

Mum took a breath and pulled the sheets back. "Look, I'm not cross with you, Maddie, I'm just worried. We're all worried. You've been spending far too much time on your own; I can't even remember the last time Gemma came over. I'd actually been thinking of taking you to see someone myself, but Mrs Palmer mentioned this nurture group she's setting up…"

"No, Mum, *please*, not the nurture group!" My heart started to race again. "I can't talk to someone I've never met before, and especially not with other people there as well. I'll try to do better at school, Mum, I promise. *Please*, I'm begging you. I'll concentrate more and—"

"Maddie, listen to me." She reached for my hand and gave it a quick squeeze. "You're going through a really tough time and I honestly don't think this is something you can sort out by yourself. If I could fix it for you, I would, but it's not going to be that easy. I can't bear seeing you like this, so quiet and withdrawn at school… struggling to sleep…missing Nan…"

"I know but—"

"Just give it a chance," she interrupted. "Don't judge it before you've tried. Sometimes it's easier to open up to a stranger, someone you've never met before."

I lay awake for ages after she left the room, thinking about the woman in the cemetery and the note she left. I remember the first week back at school in January after Nan died, Mrs Morris – our art teacher – announced a drawing competition for Year Eight. I was so excited to rush home and tell Nan that just for a moment I forgot she wouldn't be there, that I wouldn't *be able* to tell her.

I had no idea who the woman was, or how she was connected to Nan, but she would definitely understand how I was feeling right now – how difficult it was when the only person you really wanted to talk to was already dead.

4
Allergies

Vivian was younger than I was expecting. I don't know why – Vivian just sounds like an old-fashioned name. The first thing I thought when I walked into the Blue Room on Monday morning was that I'd got the wrong time, or the wrong day – she just didn't match the person I'd imagined. She had frizzy black hair pulled back with a bright red-and-yellow patterned scarf and bright-red lipstick to match.

"Hello, you must be Maddie," she said, her eyes crinkling up as she smiled. I wondered how she knew. Maybe Mrs Palmer had given her a photo of me. "I'm Vivian. Come and sit down." She waved her hand at the big table in front of her. "You're the first to arrive so take your pick."

I sat as far away from her as I could, right at the other end of the table, tucking my skirt under my legs. There was nothing much in the Blue Room – just the table and chairs, a few pieces of old work stuck up on the walls and a glossy times-tables chart. It was mostly used for maths and English booster groups, or individual special-needs sessions.

"I know there are loads of chairs out," said Vivian, "but don't worry, there are only going to be four of us, including me. Has Mrs Palmer talked to you about the nurture group at all?"

I nodded and then shook my head. Vivian laughed.

"I'm not sure if that was a yes or a no," she said. "Perhaps now would be a good time for you to ask me any questions you might have – while it's just the two of us."

I shrugged, blushing. *Who else was in the group?* That was what I really wanted to ask. I stared down at my lap, wishing I could disappear.

"It's always a bit awkward coming to something new for the first time," Vivian said gently. "We could turn it into a bit of a game if you like?"

I glanced up.

"I could ask you a question, and then you could ask

me a question. We'll take turns. You can ask me anything you like – my favourite food, my star sign, what I had for breakfast this morning. *Anything.* I'll start then, shall I?"

I shrugged again. She was trying to trick me into talking but it was never going to work; my mouth was too dry for a start, as if I'd swallowed a bucketful of sand.

"So here's my first question," said Vivian. "Do you like cats best, or dogs? They say that everyone is either a cat person or a dog person. I'm 'dog' myself. I've got a Pekinese called Sadie and she's *very* naughty." She got up and came round the table, holding her phone out to show me a picture. "She's an affectionate little thing, but stubborn as an ox."

Sadie was small with straggly hair and a funny squashed-up face. She was really cute and I couldn't help smiling.

"So how about you, Maddie? Do you like dogs?"

I nodded, still smiling.

"And how about cats?"

I nodded again.

"Oh no," said Vivian, throwing her hands up in the air. "That's against the rules. You can't say dogs *and* cats. You've got to pick one. So is it dogs or cats?"

I wasn't sure if she was joking or not. I've never had a dog *or* a cat, or any other pet for that matter. I really wanted to get a dog after Nan died. I kept thinking that if we had a puppy it might stop everyone from feeling so sad, but Mum said the dog would be stuck at home alone all day and it wouldn't be fair.

"I wanted to get a dog once," I whispered without looking up. I wasn't even sure the words had actually come out of my mouth but Vivian said, "That's great! So we're both dog people. I always know where I am with a dog person. Right, your turn, Maddie. What would you like to ask me?"

I sat there trying to think of something, but the only question I wanted to ask right at that moment was, *why did my nan have to die?* Vivian would think I was mad if I asked a question like that. I was supposed to be asking something simple, like her favourite colour or her star sign. I could hear the clock ticking on the wall. It was suddenly very loud.

"You could always write your question down, Maddie. Sometimes it's easier to write things down than say them out loud. How about I tell you a bit about the group now, and what's going to happen here, and then before you leave, if you've still got a question that you'd like to ask me, you can write it down and leave it with me. Would that be okay?"

I nodded, relieved. At least I wouldn't have to say

anything else. Vivian pushed a big, yellow pad across the table towards me.

"I adore the colour yellow," she said. "It always makes me think of the summer. I love the summer, and so does Sadie. Neither of us likes the cold very much…" She stopped for a moment, rolling her eyes. "Now look, I've told you my favourite colour *and* my favourite season."

I smiled again; I couldn't help it. Maybe she wasn't trying to trick me. Maybe she just wanted to help me feel more comfortable. I took the pad and pen and doodled a pattern across the top of the first page – a row of miniature stars shining down from the night sky. It was a relief to have something to do with my hands.

"So we're going to meet every Monday and Thursday for the next five weeks," said Vivian, "and as I mentioned a few moments ago, there will be four of us. I don't know what's happened to the other two. Perhaps they've been held up somewhere?"

Who are they? I scribbled underneath the stars. I wrote it really small so she wouldn't be able to see.

"Never mind, it's given us a chance to get to know each other a little. You're probably wondering what will actually happen while you're here…" She paused for a second, but I didn't say anything. "Well, sometimes I'll guide the sessions in a particular way, and sometimes we'll just see what comes up. I know that can sound scary, but I hope you'll come to view this room and these sessions as a safe place, Maddie. There are no expectations or pressure. You can join in as much or as little as you like, and the same goes for the other two."

Who are they? I wrote again. It was nearly twenty past nine and they still weren't here. I'd just started my next doodle – a row of tiny hearts with even smaller hearts squashed inside – when there was a knock at the door. It was a girl called Sally-Ann. She's not in my form but we have one or two classes together.

"Erm, I think I'm supposed to be in here but I'm really, *really* late," she said from the doorway.

"That's okay," said Vivian. "Come in, come in, you must be Sally-Ann. Sit wherever you like. I'm Vivian and this is Maddie."

Sally-Ann came in and plonked herself down right next to Vivian. She was small and skinny with light-brown hair.

"Hi, Maddie," she said, her eyes flicking over to me for a second. "You're in 8P aren't you? I'm in 8R." She turned back to Vivian before I could say anything. "I had a doctor's appointment this morning, that's why I'm so late. I've had this pain in my side for ages but they don't know what it is."

"How's the pain now?" asked Vivian.

"It comes and goes to be honest, but it's okay at the moment. Do you ever get that?"

I thought about the knot of anxiety I'd had in my stomach for months and months but I stared down at my pad, pretending to be busy.

"My mum thinks I'm imagining the pain," Sally-Ann went on, not really waiting for an answer. "She says it's just for attention, but she doesn't understand what it's like. I think that's why Mrs Palmer asked me to join this group, because of the pain in my side. I bet she thinks I'm making it up as well. Anyway, what have I missed?"

"Well, Maddie and I have established that we both like dogs, haven't we, Maddie?"

I could feel my face getting hot. I don't know why. Maybe it was just that Sally-Ann had said more in the last thirty seconds than I'd said during the entire meeting.

"How about you, Sally-Ann?" she went on. "Are you a dog or a cat person?"

"Oh, I really like cats but I'm allergic," she said, pushing her fringe back off her face. "I only have to sit in the same room as a cat and my eyes start streaming."

"That's a shame," said Vivian. "Allergies are such a nuisance."

They carried on talking about cats and allergies for a bit while I sat there doodling, wondering why Sally-Ann needed to come to the nurture group in the first place. She obviously didn't find it difficult to talk about her problems. She was chatting away to Vivian as if she'd known her for years.

I began to relax for the first time. The group would be so much easier with Sally-Ann here; she could do all the talking. It felt as if the pressure was off. Maybe the third person wouldn't turn up and it would just be the two of us. I wrote a couple more questions on the pad underneath my doodles. *Will I ever feel normal again? Will I ever stop worrying? Why am I so scared to talk?*

It was weird how it all started, the talking thing. It was the week I went back to school after all my time off. We were in history and Mr Bassington asked us to list the causes of the Civil War and then suddenly, without any warning at all, he called out my name. "Yes, Maddie," he said, as if my hand was *up*, as if I actually *wanted* to answer, and everyone turned to stare at me, waiting for me to speak. And even though I *knew* all the causes of the Civil War, I began to feel horribly hot and sweaty and my heart started to race and there was this massive lump in my throat...

"Do you suffer from allergies, Maddie?" said Vivian suddenly. I stopped writing and glanced up. They were both looking at me.

I shook my head. I wasn't allergic to animals or nuts or anything like that.

"Oh my god, you're so lucky," said Sally-Ann. "I'm allergic to *everything*. It's even worse at this time of year. I get the most awful hay fever."

She started to list all the things she was allergic to, counting them off on her fingers. I wanted to say I wasn't lucky at all; that I'd much rather be allergic to peanuts or pollen than have the same anxious thoughts going round and round my head on an endless loop. Everyone understands if you say you've got a nut allergy or hay fever. Sally-Ann was the lucky one.

I wrote ALLERGY right across the middle of the pad and then made a list of all the things I'd become "allergic" to since Nan died. *Coping without my purple ribbon, hospitals, talking to anyone except my family and Gemma, any kind of…*

"You're very busy there, Maddie," said Vivian. "Is it anything you'd like to share with us before we finish for today?"

I opened my mouth and closed it again, tears stinging my eyes. Mrs Palmer and Mum thought that coming to the nurture group would make everything better, but I still didn't get how talking would help – or *not* talking in my case. I shook my head again, ripping the page out of the pad and scrunching it up into a tiny ball.

"That's okay," said Vivian, as if it was no big deal. "Sometimes it helps to put things down on paper even if no one else sees." She got up and walked over to the door. "It's time to get back to class now, girls, but it's been great to meet you both."

"I'll try not to be late on Thursday," said Sally-Ann, getting up. She pressed her side and winced slightly. "Come on, Maddie, we can walk to our next class together."

I scraped my chair back and gave Vivian a small smile. I was pretty sure that coming here wouldn't make any difference to my "allergies" but I couldn't help liking her. I was just about to hand the pad back, hoping she'd let me use it again at the next session, when the door burst open.

"Oh good, this must be the third member of our group," said Vivian, stepping back.

I glanced up and then froze. I couldn't believe my eyes. It was as if someone had decided to play the worst-ever joke on me.

Vivian clasped her hands together, smiling. "Better late than never, eh, girls?" she said, giving us a little wink, and took another step back as Kieran Black strode into the room.

5

Kicking Off

I was sure it had to be a mistake – that he'd just flung the door open as he walked past the Blue Room on the way to his next lesson, but Vivian said, "Hello, Kieran, I'm Vivian. I'm so pleased we've had the chance to meet each other before Thursday."

"Where's everyone else then?" he said, his lip curling up as if there was a bad smell in the room.

"It's a small group," said Vivian. "Just you, Maddie and Sally-Ann."

Kieran looked us up and down, snorting. "I'm not coming to a group with two girls. No offence, yeah, but I'm outta here."

He swung round and was halfway through the door when Vivian said, "No offence taken. I'll look forward to seeing you on Thursday then."

He swung back round, frowning. "I said I'm not coming. Didn't you hear me?"

"We don't care, do we?" said Sally-Ann, sticking her chin in the air. "Come on, Maddie, let's go."

I was still finding it difficult to move. How could he be so rude? Vivian didn't even look cross, she just smiled her big smile and said, "It's entirely up to you, Kieran, but I do hope you'll come to the session on Thursday and tell us about the group you were *hoping* to find when you opened the door. Unfortunately we're out of time for today, so we'll have to say goodbye for now."

I thought Kieran was going to explode. I hunched my shoulders and half-closed my eyes, convinced he was going to shout at Vivian, or worse, but a beat later it was over. You could almost feel the fight go out of him. Somehow Vivian had managed to get the last word. He turned and slunk out of the room, muttering to himself, his hands thrust deep in his pockets.

Sally-Ann flounced out after him and I followed behind, keeping my head down, eyes fixed on the ground, relieved the whole thing was over and done with.

Gemma was waiting for me by my locker, scanning the

corridor. "Where have you been?" she said as I came towards her. "You missed registration."

I waved my hand vaguely in the direction of the Blue Room and muttered something about a meeting. I couldn't face telling her I'd been to a special counselling session – she'd want to know why I didn't tell her before, and what it was for, and who else was in the group, and I still had no idea how I was supposed to explain.

"What sort of meeting?" she said, glancing back over my shoulder as if she was trying to work it out. "Was it something to do with the summer fair?"

"No, nothing like that," I said, tugging at her arm. "Come on, we need to go – the bell's about to ring."

There was no sign of Kieran when we got to English. He usually walks in late, if he bothers turning up at all. Gemma grabbed two seats at the front where she always sits, but I decided it would be safer at the back – less chance of Miss Owen calling on me or asking me to read my work out. Gemma gave me a funny look, pointing at the chair next to her, but I bit my lip, shrugging. I knew she'd be upset, but sitting at the front felt too risky.

We were supposed to be finishing our autobiographies but I couldn't stop thinking about Vivian and the group. A part of me had already decided I was never going back, but there was something about the way she'd handled

Kieran Black, the way she stood her ground without shouting at him or showing any fear. I'd never seen a teacher deal with Kieran like that before. He was always either thrown out of class or put in detention.

He finally turned up ten minutes before the end of the lesson, flinging the door open so it slammed back against the wall.

"Where on earth have you been?" asked Miss Owen, rolling her eyes and looking at her watch. "I'm really struggling to see the point of you walking in to my lesson when there's so little time left..."

Kieran curled his lip, sneering at her. It was obvious he couldn't care less whether Miss Owen could see the point or not. Gemma turned round and caught my eye, making a loser sign with her hand. I stared down at my book, my face burning up. It would be so embarrassing if she found out that Kieran and I were having counselling sessions *together*.

He dragged his bag up the aisle towards the back of the room, bending down as he passed my chair to whisper *"Maddie Mouse"* in my ear. I kept my eyes on my book, chewing the end of my pen, waiting for my face to cool down. Nan used to say that everyone had something good inside them, however hard they tried to hide it – but then she never met Kieran Black.

* * *

It was packed in the cafeteria at lunch. I picked at my chicken-and-mayo sandwich while Gemma filled me in on what I'd missed at registration. Apparently Mrs Palmer had announced a new after-school rounders club for Year Eights but I was only half-listening. A girl sitting right in front of us had a bright blue lunch box, the exact colour of the scarf the woman in the cemetery was wearing yesterday. I really needed to see her again, to ask her about the note, to find out who she was and how she knew Nan...

"It starts on Wednesday with Mr Skinner," Gemma said, shaking my arm to get my attention. "I thought I might join actually. What do you think, Mads, shall we do it together?"

I shook my head, trying to focus. "I've never played rounders before. We didn't do it at primary school."

"Come on, Maddie, *please*, it sounds really good. I wish you'd tell me what's wrong. You never want to do anything any more!"

Just then I noticed Kieran come into the canteen. I dropped my head as he scanned the room, praying he wouldn't see me. I just didn't get why Mrs Palmer thought it would be a good idea to put me in a group with someone like him. A *nurture* group. How could something be nurturing with Kieran Black there? It was crazy.

"So what *was* your meeting about if it wasn't the summer fair?" said Gemma suddenly, as if she could read my mind. "I asked Mrs Palmer but she basically told me to mind my own business."

"It was a kind of assessment thing," I said, only half-lying. "About my progress this term…"

"Oh right, what happened? You weren't in trouble, were you? Do you need me to help you with anything? Maths homework? Science?"

"No, it was nothing like that. Okay, listen, I'll come to rounders if you really want me to."

I only said it to change the subject. I just didn't know *how* to talk to her about the nurture group, it felt too private to discuss, especially the majorly embarrassing fact that Kieran was part of it.

Gemma took a bite of her sandwich, watching me, waiting to see if I was going to say anything else. She probably realized I was dodging her questions, putting her off, lying to her.

"Do you know Nathan Meyer in 8B?" she said after a bit.

I shook my head.

"He lives on my road. Look, he's over there." She

58

pointed across the canteen at a crowd of boys on another table.

I shook my head again and frowned, not sure what this Nathan had to do with anything. "I've seen him around but I don't really know him, why?"

"No reason," she said, getting frustrated. "You wouldn't understand anyway." She scraped her chair back, stuffing the rest of her sandwich in her bag. "I've got to go. It's maths club and I don't want to be late."

I watched as she rushed out of the canteen without even saying bye. It was as if she was letting me know she could keep secrets too. I wanted to run after her. To tell her I was sorry, to ask what it was she wanted to tell me about Nathan. I really wanted things to go back to how they used to be. But it was like a wall was growing between us and I had no idea how to knock it down.

We have art last thing on Mondays with Mrs Morris. It's easily my favourite class of the week. It's in a big, sunny studio at the top of the school, every centimetre of the walls covered in paintings, pictures and sketches – every spare table crammed with half-finished models made out of clay and modroc: our *works in progress*, as Mrs Morris likes to call them.

I feel different when I'm in the art room. There's something about drawing and painting and modelling that stops me thinking about Nan or Kieran Black or anything. I get so absorbed in my work it's like being transported to a different place, a quiet place, where I don't have to worry about anything except the piece of work in front of me.

We've been doing portraiture this term. Gemma and I have been working on ours together. She's been painting my face from a photo and I've been doing hers using tiny pieces of torn-up newspaper. We only started a couple of weeks before half-term but it's a brilliant topic, one of my favourites so far this year.

I could see Gemma over by the sink, mixing paint. We hadn't spoken since lunch, since she mentioned that boy Nathan and rushed off to maths club. It's PE before art, but we're in different sets. I grabbed a pile of newspaper, ready to make a start on her hair, wondering if she was still upset. She usually waits for me outside the changing rooms but she must've come straight up to the art room. It would be awful if she didn't want us to be partners any more.

"Quick, take one of these, Mads," she said a minute later, staggering over with three different pots and a load of brushes. "I literally can't wait to see how you're going to do my plaits!"

I shifted up to make room for her on the bench,

massively relieved. I knew it was her way of saying we were okay again. She never stays cross for long – but I had a horrible feeling she wouldn't keep forgiving me for ever, not if I kept keeping secrets and pushing her away.

Most of the class were working together in pairs, chatting about their portraits, helping each other as they went along. I'm usually one hundred per cent focused in art – a bomb could drop and I wouldn't notice – but for some reason my eyes kept wandering over to Kieran. He was sitting by himself at the back of the room, his head bent over his picture. I wasn't sure if he'd chosen to work by himself, or if no one else wanted to pair up with him.

"Help me a minute, would you?" said Gemma, nudging me. "I can't get your nose right and it's driving me nuts."

I was about to turn back round to show her my nose when Kieran glanced up and caught me staring. Our eyes locked for a second, then a nasty smile spread across his face as he lifted his hands up to the sides of his mouth to make mousy whiskers.

I dropped my head, my cheeks flaming. Why did he keep doing that? Treating me like I was the world's biggest joke? I tried to stay focused on my work for the rest of the lesson, shredding tiny pieces of newspaper to make individual strands of hair. I didn't dare look round again, but I could feel his eyes burning into the back of my head.

As soon as the bell rang I slipped out of class and hurried towards my locker to get my stuff. All I could think about was that I hated Kieran Black, and I hated the fact that Mrs Palmer had lumped us together in Vivian's special group as if we were the same. Did she really think that forcing me to sit in a room with someone like him twice a week was going to help me talk or improve my grades?

I was out of school and halfway down Banner Road when I heard Gemma calling my name. I hadn't even thought of her in my rush to get away from Kieran.

"Hang on a minute!" she yelled, running to catch up. "Why did you disappear like that, without saying bye? What's the matter?"

"Nothing, I'm fine."

"Oh, right." She fixed me with a look. "Well I was just wondering if you wanted to come back to mine for a bit. I could help you with your history topic…"

I hesitated for a moment, scuffing my foot on the pavement. How could I explain that I needed to go straight to the cemetery? That I was hoping the woman in the blue scarf might be there?

"Um…I haven't actually got my project with me," I said, dodging her gaze. "I haven't even—"

"Look, why don't you just say you don't want to hang out?" she interrupted, her eyes blazing. "I'm not stupid. You've been acting weird with me for ages."

"I do," I said. "I *do* want to hang out. It's not *you*, Gemma. It's just…" I searched for the right words, a way to make her understand how messed up everything was: missing Nan, the nurture group, *Kieran Black*. "I'm just… I'm just not feeling very well…"

"I thought you said you were fine just now? God, Maddie, you're not the only one with problems, you know!"

"I know, I'm sorry. Please, Gem, it's not you."

I reached out for her arm, but she pushed me away and took off down the road without looking back. I wanted to go after her, to say sorry again – I knew I was hurting her, pushing her away, making her feel like I didn't want to hang out any more, but I couldn't help it. Something much stronger was drawing me in the opposite direction, down Banner Road and towards the cemetery.

It was pretty much deserted when I got there, just an old man by the entrance reading the paper. A part of me knew the woman wouldn't turn up – and that even if she did I'd probably be too scared to say anything – but I had to wait for her just in case. Almost as if, in a weird sort of way, she was my last ever link to Nan.

* * *

Mum asked me about the nurture group later that evening. We were in the kitchen and she was busy making a salad for dinner. She wanted to know what Vivian was like and who else was there and what we'd talked about and if I thought it was going to help – firing the questions at me like bullets, one after the other.

"You did go, didn't you, Maddie?" she said, after I'd shrugged a few times.

"I did, but I really don't want to go back on Thursday."

"What do you mean?" She stopped mid-slice. "You've got to go, it's important. I thought you understood. What was it? Was it Vivian? Didn't you like her?"

"No, Vivian was nice," I said, trying to make her understand. "It's just there's this boy in the group, Kieran Black."

Something flickered across Mum's face. "*Kieran Black?*"

"Why are you saying it like that? You don't know him, do you?"

She shook her head. "I used to know his mum, Samantha, but I didn't know her son was in your year."

"He's not just in my year, he's in my form. He joined Church Vale in January."

I'd never mentioned Kieran to Mum before or told her

about him picking on me all the time. I was scared she might go up to school and make a big fuss – that it would end up making things worse. She turned back to the salad and started to slice up some cherry tomatoes. She was stalling, it was so obvious.

"Come on, why did you say it like that?" I said. "Why did you make that face? Is it his mum? How did you know her?"

She hesitated before she spoke. "No, it's not his mum, Maddie – it's…it's…nothing. Just forget I said anything, okay?"

"You can't just tell me to forget it. I hate it when you do that. Is it something to do with work?"

"Well, I have been involved with his family at work," she said slowly, "but you know I can't discuss it with you."

Mum's a specialist nurse at an addiction clinic, helping people who are trying to give up drugs or alcohol. Everything that happens there is strictly confidential and she never tells me anything, but it was obvious from the way she was acting that Kieran's mum must be one of her patients.

She turned the tap on to wash the cucumber. "So what's this Kieran like? Is he nice?"

"Horrible," I said, without hesitating. "Everyone hates him. That's why I'm not going back to the group."

"Has he ever done anything horrible to you?"

I nodded, thinking of the drum roll, the way he was always winding me up, calling me Maddie Mouse.

"He hasn't hurt you, has he?"

"No, nothing like that. He's just a pain."

Mum turned back to face me, her head tipped to one side. "Lots of people are a pain, Maddie. I don't honestly think that's a reason to stop going to the nurture group. I mean you could look at it in a completely different way…"

"What do you mean?"

"Well, you need some help coming to terms with losing your nan, and perhaps Kieran needs some help fitting in to Church Vale, learning how to make friends?"

"*Mum!*" I said, getting annoyed. "*You* sound like a counsellor now. You don't know what he's like – he's a nightmare! And anyway, no one can help me come to terms with losing Nan. Not Vivian or you or *anyone*. You weren't there when it happened. You don't know what *that* was like either. I'll *never* come to terms with it and there's nothing you can do to make me!"

Mum opened her mouth to say something but just at that moment the phone rang. We both froze, our eyes locked across the room.

"Don't go anywhere," she said, picking up the phone.

"I haven't finished with you. I'm sorry, Mads, but I'm not letting this go."

As soon as Mum started speaking I realized it was Sharon, the woman who'd rung up for Dad last week after school. I could only hear Mum's side of the conversation, but it was exactly the same conversation she'd had with me. Mum wrote down the number and said goodbye, and then she just stood there with a puzzled look on her face, as if she was trying to work out a really difficult sum in her head.

I edged towards the door, pleased for the chance to escape.

Mum glanced up at me.

"Hang on a minute, Maddie," she said before I could slip away. "I wasn't joking. I want you to carry on with the nurture group and that's my final word on the subject."

"Okay," I said, but with my fingers crossed tightly behind my back. There was no way I was going to the next session however much she wanted me to, and that was *my* final word on the subject.

6
Sharon

Mum didn't mention Sharon or the phone call again until the following evening. Charlie was in the garden kicking the ball against the wall and Mum and I were in the kitchen tiptoeing around each other, both of us avoiding the subject of the nurture group in case it sparked off another row.

"There's only three of us tonight," she said, just as I finished laying the table. "Sorry, Mads, I forgot to say, Dad's not coming home."

"What do you mean? Where is he?"

"He's gone to meet Sharon," said Mum. "She rang up for him yesterday, remember? Call Charlie in, would you, love, I don't want him overdoing it. Dinner's ready anyway and I'm trying out a new recipe."

Charlie came crashing in from the garden, hot and sweaty, muttering something about his shots and how much better they were getting. He'd been outside every spare minute since the football letters went out, determined to get picked for the next match. He said Mr Maddox was always swapping the team around, trying out new players.

"So who *is* this Sharon then?" I asked as soon as we were all sitting down. "I thought Dad said he didn't know anyone called Sharon when she called the first time?"

"Oh, she's just someone he used to go out with years and years ago."

"Wowee, sexy!" said Charlie, pulling a funny face and jiggling his eyebrows up and down.

Mum burst out laughing. "Don't be daft! It's not like that now. They're just old friends."

She was trying to sound casual, too casual, as if it was no big deal.

"But I don't understand," I said. "How can they be old friends if he said he didn't even know her? How can you just *forget* a friend? And Dad hardly ever goes out in the week by himself; he always says he'd much rather be home with us…"

"Maddie, stop going on, will you? I feel like I'm being

cross-examined. Dad rang her back yesterday evening, and as soon as he spoke to her he realized who she was. It's difficult to remember sometimes after so many years. Anyway, she said she needed to talk to him about something, so he's gone to meet her for a quick drink and that's it. Now no more questions, okay?"

"Can I just ask you something, Mum?" said Charlie. "Why are there pears in my chicken?"

Dad didn't get back until really late. His quick drink must've turned into a very slow one. I lay in bed, wide awake, trying to imagine him and Sharon in the pub together, chatting about old times. She was probably tall and blonde, with long eyelashes and loads of make-up. The exact opposite of Mum.

As soon as I heard his key in the door I crept out of bed and stood at the top of the stairs, my ribbon clutched tight in my hand.

"What are you doing awake?" he whispered as he came up.

He looked strange in the dim glow of the hall light; his eyes were red and puffy. I twisted my ribbon round and round my finger, wondering if he'd been crying. I'd never seen Dad cry before, not even at Nan's funeral.

"I'm sorry, I just wanted to say goodnight. I couldn't sleep."

He wrapped his arms round me and held me close.

"You missed chicken-and-pear bake," I said into his chest. "Charlie nearly threw up."

Dad laughed quietly, holding me even tighter. "Don't ever forget how much I love you, Maddie Wilkins," he said.

"Why would I forget? What's the matter?"

"Nothing's the matter, sweetheart. It's just sometimes you realize how lucky you are. Now off to bed. You'll be shattered in the morning." He kissed the top of my head. "Go on, it's nearly midnight."

I lay in bed listening to him and Mum talk through my bedroom wall. I couldn't make out what they were saying, but I figured it had to be about Sharon. My tummy was in knots trying to work out what it could all mean. Why had she bothered to get in touch with Dad after so many years? And why had he come home in such a strange mood?

He seemed to be fine in the morning; his eyes weren't red or puffy any more, he just looked totally worn out. He promised Charlie he'd be home in time to do some football practice, grabbed a slice of toast and went straight outside to get his tools ready for work.

"Is Dad okay?" I asked Mum as soon as he'd left the room.

"What do you mean? Why wouldn't he be?"

"It's just he got back really late and—"

"I know, Maddie Wilkins," she interrupted, turning to face me, her hands on her hips. "And I *also* happen to know you were still up and out of your room. How on earth do you expect to start concentrating at school if you never get to sleep at a normal time? Honestly, Mads, Dad's fine – *everything's* fine – so there's absolutely *nothing* for you to worry about!"

It was the first rounders session after school. I was praying Gemma might forget or change her mind but as soon as the bell rang at the end of the day she dragged me off to get changed. I'd lied to her about never playing before; we used to play at primary school and I was okay. I just couldn't face joining in with anything at the moment.

Mr Skinner was waiting for us on the field, setting up the bases. There were about twenty other Year Eights, but no sign of Kieran Black – thank goodness. I sat right at the side while Mr Skinner went through the rules a couple of times and then divided us into teams. I nearly said I was only there to watch, but I didn't want to risk upsetting Gemma again, not after the other day.

Our team was batting first, so we got in line with the others, as near to the back as we could, and then sat on the grass waiting for our turn. A girl called Annika was at the front. She looked really sporty – short shorts, tight T-shirt, expensive trainers, but the ball flew straight past her before she could even lift the bat.

"Oh my god! I'm rubbish!" she squealed and burst out laughing, half skipping, half running to first base, flapping her arms around like a bird. A few of the others groaned and rolled their eyes but she didn't seem to be bothered.

"Keep your eye on the ball, Annika," Mr Skinner called out. "And don't forget to drop the bat!"

Annika chucked the bat back and the next person on our team went up. It was Nathan, the boy Gemma had pointed out to me in the canteen the other day. He turned to give us all a thumbs up and someone shouted, "Come on, Nate!" It was obvious he knew what he was doing. He pulled his arm back and whacked the ball so far he was able to run all the way round the four bases with time to spare, scoring the first rounder. We all cheered and a few of our team went over to high-five him.

"I'll never be able to hit it," muttered Gemma. "I'm useless at ball games."

"Why did you want to come then? It was your idea!"

She blushed bright red. "I know, I know, I just wanted to do something apart from studying all the time."

Finally it was her turn. She slipped her glasses off, flicked her plaits over her shoulders and raised the bat, ready.

"Good luck," I said. "Keep your eye on the ball!"

She blinked a few times squinting into the sun and then raised her hand up to shield her eyes as the ball sailed straight past her. "Oh no! What do I do now?" she cried, dropping the bat and then picking it up, and then dropping it again. The fielders burst out laughing which gave her the chance to run. She looked back at me from first base, crossing her fingers for luck as I went up to bat next.

The field looked huge suddenly. I tried not to think of everyone watching me, waiting to see if I was any good. My heart began to speed up. It was just like the other day when Miss Owen asked me to read out my autobiography. I had an overwhelming urge to run away and hide but it was as if someone had cemented my feet to the ground.

Larissa Morris from our form was bowling. I squinted across the grass, past her and the other fielders, through the glaring sunlight, and just for a split second, where the field ends and the sycamore trees begin, I thought I could make out Nan. Not in a scary way. Not like a proper, solid person – just the shape of her: a rough, smudgy outline like one of my sketches.

A warm feeling flooded my belly, like the sun was inside me, and even though it was too far away to see her face I knew she was smiling. I shut everything else out, squashed down my anxiety and focused on the ball as it came hurtling through the air towards me. There was a loud crack and Larissa ducked down as it flew over her head and deep into the field.

"Run!" I shouted to Gemma as I dropped the bat and took off towards first base.

"Don't stop!" yelled Nate, as I raced round, past first and on to second.

I only managed to get as far as third base before the fielders got the ball and threw it to Larissa, but it felt amazing. I couldn't believe it. I'd hit the ball! But not only that – I'd shouted "*run*" in front of all the others without even thinking.

I glanced back at the row of sycamore trees, searching for the smudgy outline through the glare of the sun, but there was nothing there.

"Well done, Maddie!" Mr Skinner called out. "Great hit!"

And then everyone was looking at Abdul, the next

person up to bat, and I turned towards fourth base, a massive grin on my face, ready to run again.

"You were brilliant!" said Gemma when I got back to her. "Why didn't you tell me how good you were? I thought you'd never played rounders before?"

Just then Nathan came over to talk to us about fielding. Gemma went bright red again, stammering something about her weak wrists and not being very good at catching.

"No worries," he said. "I'll be bowling so just keep your eye on the ball and pass it back to me as soon as you get it."

She stared up at him, nodding, as if he'd just explained the meaning of life and I wondered if she liked him, if that was the *real* reason she'd been so keen for us to join. I almost asked her, but I thought she might be embarrassed if I just blurted it out – we've never really talked about boys before, not about *liking* them.

The other team scored three-and-a-half rounders and then it was our turn to bat again. We were easily better than them and the final score was 10–6 to us; mostly thanks to Nathan. Gemma talked about him all the way down Banner Road, about how good he was at batting and how fast he could run, and how pleased she was that we'd joined.

She thanked me at least a million times for agreeing to come and said she couldn't wait for next Wednesday.

"Seven days, Maddie," she sighed, as if it was seven years.

But I was looking forward to it too. I'd got so caught up in the game after my first go at batting I'd hardly thought about anything except throwing and catching and hitting and running for a whole hour.

7
Photos in the Attic

I spotted Dad's van as soon as I turned into our road: bright blue with *Wilkins Electrical Services* splashed across the side. It was weird to see it parked outside the house so early. Dad's never usually home before six. His final job of the day must've been cancelled – either that or something was wrong.

I let myself in and called out, but the house felt empty. He wasn't in the kitchen or the lounge. I dropped my bag and raced upstairs calling out again, my tummy starting to churn. Why was his van outside if he wasn't in? Where else could he be? It didn't make any sense. At the top of the stairs I noticed a narrow shaft of light shining down from the trapdoor to the attic.

We hardly ever use our attic for anything except storing junk. Mum always says she can't face going up there because she knows what a terrible mess it's in. I climbed the old, rickety ladder and pulled myself up through the hole in the ceiling. It was dark and gloomy, difficult to see through the dust even with the light switched on.

Dad was sitting in the middle of the floor surrounded by a load of old photo albums.

"*Maddie!*" He jumped slightly and started to gather the albums up as if I'd caught him doing something wrong. "You startled me. I didn't realize you were back..."

"Didn't you hear me? I called up."

"Sorry, love, I was miles away."

He looked exhausted, as if he was coming down with something. I used to think my dad was invincible, like a superhero; that nothing could ever happen to him, but not any more. I picked my way across the bare floorboards and kneeled down in front of him. "How come you're home so early? What are you doing?"

"Nothing really. Just sorting through a few of these old photos. It's difficult to stop once you start – so many memories..."

There was a small pile of photos on the floor. I picked it up and had a quick look through the pictures as my eyes adjusted to the gloom. The first one was of me, Charlie and Nan at the Natural History Museum. We're standing in front of this huge T. rex, both of us clutching hold of Nan's hands as if we're scared it might actually come to life behind us.

There was another one of me and Charlie on our own. I must've been about six and Charlie two. He's sitting on my lap and I've got my arms wrapped around him, holding him in place. I can't believe how small he looks; he's got a dummy in his mouth and he's wearing a blue and white striped sleepsuit, the sort you wear when you're a tiny baby.

I glanced up at Dad. "Why have you taken these out of the albums? Is it…is it because of Nan?"

Dad looked at me, confused, as if I was speaking a different language. I carried on, flustered. "I mean were you looking for some old photos of Nan? Is that why you came up here?"

Dad's hardly mentioned Nan at all since she died – not to me in any case – almost as if he buried all his memories of her on the day of the funeral.

I wondered how he'd react if I told him about rounders, about seeing her by the sycamore trees – how she'd helped me whack the ball across the field. He'd probably make a big joke out of it; say it sounded as if I'd had a whack to my *head,* never mind the ball. Sometimes I wonder if he even thinks about her any more.

"Look at this one," he said, handing me another photo. It was Nan blowing out the candles on her sixtieth birthday. She's leaning down and the glow from the tiny flames has made a kind of golden halo around her head. Charlie's standing next to her with a plate in his hand, ready to grab the first slice. I remember Nan laughing about the number of candles and how there wouldn't be enough room on the cake if she made it to seventy.

"Can we put this up somewhere? We could get a nice frame for it."

"Of course we can, and some of these as well," he said, holding his hand out for the rest of the photos. "I can't see the point of them gathering dust up here where no one can see them." He shoved the albums back in a box and pulled me up. "Come on, let's go down. Mum and Charlie will be back any second and I could murder a cup of tea."

It was brilliant having Dad home early. He played football with Charlie in the garden and then sat with me for ages while I struggled through my maths homework; one simultaneous equation after another. I couldn't remember ever finding maths so difficult before – it was like someone had mixed up all the wires in my brain.

I could tell Dad was surprised; he didn't say anything but I caught him looking over my head at Mum a few times.

But then, right before dinner, Dad said he was just nipping out, grabbed his jacket and disappeared. When I asked Mum about it, she said he was meeting Sharon *again*, but she didn't laugh this time, not even when Charlie started to jiggle his eyebrows. Apparently Sharon needed Dad's help with something but Mum couldn't discuss it with us because it was grown-up stuff and we wouldn't understand.

I hate it when she says that, as if Charlie and I are the same age. *He* might be too young but why couldn't she tell *me* what was going on? I watched her carefully all through dinner, trying to work out if she was upset or worried, but she hardly said a word. As soon as we'd finished eating and everything was cleared away, she sent us both up to bed.

"We all need an early night," she said firmly, "and I don't want any arguments."

I lay in bed for hours, curled up on my side, watching the numbers change on my clock, my ribbon twisted round my hand. I knew I wouldn't fall asleep until I heard Dad's key in the door, until I knew he was home. I wanted to ask him about the woman in the cemetery anyway. I was still desperate to find out who she was and why she left that note saying sorry, and I hoped that Dad might have the answers.

I thought about writing my own note to Nan. Vivian said it can help to put things down on paper even if no one else sees. I could tell her how Mum tried to make an apple and blueberry crumble using her own recipe but it came out all wrong – that Nan was the only one who knew how to make it exactly the way I liked.

Mum came into my room at one point to check on me. I hid my ribbon under the pillow so she wouldn't see and pretended to be asleep. She used to think it was cute when I was little – Maddie and her purple ribbon – but not any more. Now it's just something to nag me about – something I should've outgrown years ago, like Charlie sucking his thumb.

It was only after she'd gone, and I was still lying there awake, that I realized Dad never actually explained *why* he'd come home so early, or why he was up in the attic going through all the old photos. And then I realized something else. I had no idea if it meant anything or if it was just a coincidence, but once the thought was in my head it was impossible to get it out.

There were photos of me and Charlie and Dad and Nan in the special pile he'd made, but not a single one of Mum.

* * *

I must've dropped off in the end because the next thing I knew it was morning and my alarm was ringing. I jumped out of bed and threw on my uniform. What if Dad wasn't back yet? What if he'd stayed out all night? What if he'd been taken ill? I tried to remember if Dad had *ever* stayed out all night, apart from when Charlie was in hospital, but I couldn't think of a single time.

I was fumbling with my tie, my fingers like sausages, when Charlie came bursting into my room. "Breakfast's ready," he said. "Mum said hurry up or you'll be late."

"Is Dad back?"

He gave me a funny look. "Of course he is! Come on, Maddie, hurry up, it's pancakes! Mum said to tell you it's a special treat and you'll miss them if you don't come straight down!"

Dad was standing right in the middle of the kitchen with the frying pan in his hand, about to toss the first pancake in the air.

"Stand back, Mads," he said, as if it was a perfectly normal morning. "You know I don't have the best track record when it comes to this!"

Charlie was jumping up and down, so excited you'd think it was Christmas.

"Do it! Do it!" he cried. "Come on, Dad. I'm *starving!*"

No one mentioned Sharon or how late Dad got back or

where he'd been, or how we *never* normally have pancakes on a school day. It was just "Pass the lemon", and "Can I have more sugar?" And "No, Mum, I do *not* want sliced pears on my pancake". I began to relax a little. Dad was home and nothing terrible had happened. I ate my pancake with a big squeeze of lemon and lots of sugar, trying as hard as I could to enjoy the moment.

Jumping In!

I thought I'd decided one hundred per cent that I wasn't going back to the nurture group for the second session, but when I got to school my legs seemed to lead me to the Blue Room as if they had a life of their own. Sally-Ann was already sitting down but I was relieved to see there was no sign of Kieran.

Vivian waited for me to take my seat and then pushed the yellow pad towards me. "It's entirely up to you, Maddie, but just in case you feel like writing anything down…"

"Oh my god, I hate writing," said Sally-Ann. "It's so boring. I had this teacher at primary school who used to force us to write a long story every Friday afternoon, just when we were the most fed up and tired. It was a total nightmare. I started to get…"

Suddenly the door flew open and Kieran walked in, his hands thrust deep in his pockets. I stared down at the pad, determined not to make eye contact, doodling my name across the top of the page.

"Hello, Kieran," said Vivian. "Sally-Ann was just telling us about how much she hates writing."

"I was just going to say that I started to get the worst stomach ache every Friday," Sally-Ann went on. "It was so bad that one time my mum had to come and pick me up, but then my friend Shelley told the teacher that I was making it up just so I could get out of writing my story and my mum was furious. I hated Shelley after that; I never spoke to her again!"

"It doesn't sound as if she was a very good friend," said Vivian. "I hope you've got some better friends here at Church Vale."

"I have. I've got three best friends – Tara, Rachel and Amina. Tara's actually the best friend I've ever had. We tell each other *everything*."

I glanced across the table at Kieran. He'd taken five small stones out of his pocket and he was trying to balance them one on top of the other. Vivian and Sally-Ann were still talking about Sally-Ann's friends and how close they were. I doodled the word FRIEND across my pad and then wrote GEMMA all the way round in tiny letters, over and over, until I'd written her name at least twenty times.

"How about you, Maddie?" said Vivian. "Do you have a good friend at Church Vale?"

I nodded and then shook my head, confused suddenly, not sure how to answer.

"I thought you and Gemma Summers were best friends?" said Sally-Ann, pushing her fringe out of her eyes. "You're always hanging out together."

"And how about you, Kieran?" said Vivian before I could explain about Gemma – about how we used to tell each other everything, just like Sally-Ann and Tara, but that she didn't even know I was part of the nurture group or how much my grades had slipped or how anxious I'd been feeling – that it was the first time I'd ever kept secrets from her.

Kieran raised his head slowly to look at Vivian.

"Oh I've got loads of friends," he said, sneering. "Haven't you heard? I'm the most popular boy in Year Eight."

"That's nice," said Vivian, as if she actually believed him. "It's great to be popular, although I always think it's quality that matters when it comes to friends rather than quantity, do you know what I mean?"

I had no idea who she was asking – me, Sally-Ann or Kieran – but Sally-Ann said, "You mean it's better to have one or two close friends than loads of superficial friends."

"Do you agree with that, Kieran?" said Vivian. "About quality being more important than quantity?"

"I'm only here because I have to be," said Kieran. "I don't have to talk to you if I don't want to."

Vivian smiled at him. She was so pretty. I wondered if she had a boyfriend or if she lived on her own with her dog Sadie.

"You're absolutely right about that, Kieran," she said. "You don't have to do anything in here that you don't want to."

He glared at her as if he'd half-wanted her to say he *did* have to talk and then went back to balancing his stones. I watched him more closely. His whole body was tensed up as if he expected the ceiling to fall in at any moment, his face pale and pinched under his dark, messy hair. He took each stone and lowered it carefully onto the one below, and then just when he'd managed to balance all five, he knocked them down again so that they scattered across the table.

"Hey, watch it!" said Sally-Ann, and she flicked the stones back across the table. He grabbed them up and shoved them in his pocket, slumping so far down in his chair that only his head was visible.

"So Sally-Ann's got three best friends and Kieran's got loads," said Vivian, turning to me. "Do you have any close friends *outside* of Church Vale, Maddie?"

I stared down at the pad, scribbling over what I'd written. I didn't know what to say. They were all looking at me, waiting. Sweat dripped down my back, the panicky feeling rising up in my chest. I quickly wrote something about my old neighbour Grace who went to live in Australia and pushed the pad across the table to Vivian.

"Oh, that must be difficult," she said glancing down and then passing it back to me. "Australia is so far away. Do you keep in touch?"

I nodded, wishing she would stop asking me questions. Grace and I still emailed each other sometimes, but we'd never really been that close. I hadn't actually thought about her in ages.

"Maybe she'll come to visit some time?" said Vivian.

"I wouldn't come to visit England if I lived in Australia," said Sally-Ann. "It's so much better than here."

"Shame you *don't* live there then," muttered Kieran.

"Shame *you* don't," Sally-Ann shot back.

They glared at each other across the table.

"Yes, well, sometimes we have to get on with the

people we're stuck with," said Vivian calmly, "even if at times we'd prefer them to live on the other side of the world."

Sally-Ann made a face at Kieran but he was fiddling around with his stones.

"The thing is, Maddie," said Vivian, turning back to me. "If you've made one good friend then I'm sure you'll make another. It's a bit like riding a bike – once you've learned how, you never forget."

I shrugged and looked back down at the pad. I already had a special friend – but if I wasn't careful I'd end up pushing her away.

"Although it *can* feel scary," Vivian went on. "It's a bit like jumping into a freezing-cold swimming pool. I've always thought you can learn a lot about people by the way they get into a swimming pool."

We all looked up at her. It was such a random thing to say.

"Haven't you ever noticed the way some people spend ages dipping their toes and then going in up to their knees, squealing like babies at every step – while other people jump straight in without giving it a second thought."

"But what's that got to do with making friends?" said Sally-Ann.

"Well it's not just to do with making friends," said Vivian. "It's anything we're scared of really. You see once a 'dipper' actually gets into the water and realizes how gorgeous it is, they often end up wondering why it took them so long in the first place…"

"Who cares?" said Kieran. "And who cares about making friends? This is crap!" He scraped his chair back and walked out, slamming the door behind him.

I held my breath waiting to see what Vivian would do, but she carried on as if it hadn't happened. "It's time to wrap things up for the day, anyway," she said. "Thank you for coming, girls, I've really enjoyed the session."

"I might not be here on Monday," said Sally-Ann. "I've got a hospital appointment. It's because my allergies are so bad at the moment."

"Oh that's a shame. I hope your appointment goes well and I'll see you next Thursday."

I hung back for a second until Sally-Ann had gone so I could hand the pad back to Vivian. I had a sudden urge to talk to her on my own. To tell her how much I was still missing Nan, and about Dad meeting up with Sharon and the pile of old photos, and how I was too scared to tell Gemma I was part of the nurture group. How every day at the moment felt like jumping straight into a freezing-cold swimming pool, but not in a good way.

"Thank you, Maddie," she said, taking the pad. "How did you find the session today?"

I opened my mouth and closed it again, my heart starting to beat against my chest like a trapped bird. I couldn't do it. I couldn't get the words out. It was so frustrating. "It's just...it's just..." I trailed off, staring down at the floor. Why was it *so* difficult for me to talk about how I was really feeling?

"New things are always hard at the beginning," Vivian said, gently. "It'll get easier, I promise. There's no rush."

Gemma was waiting for me outside. "Is this where you meet then? In the Blue Room? I didn't realize this assessment stuff was going to be a regular thing."

I nodded, embarrassed. I wondered how long she'd been standing there – if she'd seen Kieran storm out. I was about to make up some excuse, to say he wasn't really part of the group, but she was busy opening her bag to show me her history project on the English Civil War. I could see it was good without even looking at it properly; she must've spent hours on it.

"I know it's not due in until Monday but I'm going to hand it in today so I can do the rest of my homework at the weekend. Hey, rounders was cool, wasn't it?"

"Yeah, really cool," I said, only half-listening. I was still thinking about what Vivian said, about the swimming pool and being too scared to jump in, wondering if she was right and it really would get easier – if one day I'd feel the way I did before Nan had her stroke.

We have double English on Thursdays. We'd finished autobiographies and were starting a new unit on *Holes* by Louis Sachar.

"Camp Green Lake is a place for *bad* boys," said Miss Owen as a way of introducing the book.

My eyes went straight to Kieran. I couldn't help it. I've read *Holes* and if one person from the whole of Year Eight was going to be sent to Camp Green Lake it would definitely be Kieran Black. He was sitting at the back, balancing his stones again. I knew Miss Owen wouldn't tell him to put them away or anything. She'd just be relieved he wasn't disrupting her lesson.

After reading the first few chapters we had to discuss and then write down our impressions of Stanley Yelnats, the main character. He wasn't actually "bad" at all. He was picked on at school, bullied by the other kids *and* the teachers. Teased about his size. I felt sorry for him. It wasn't his fault he got into trouble; he was just in the wrong place at the wrong time.

Miss Owen started to call on people to share their thoughts. I kept my head down, praying she wouldn't choose me. I had loads of ideas but the bird was back in my chest, flapping its wings, beating against my ribs. I half-closed my eyes, convinced she was about to say my name, wishing I had my purple ribbon with me, when Kieran stood up suddenly, knocking his chair over behind him.

"Yes, Mr Black, can I help you?" said Miss Owen, the sarcasm dripping off her tongue.

I thought he was going to say something sarcastic back like he usually did, but he shook his head, his face deathly white, his eyes bright with tears. I wondered for a minute if he was ill, if he was about to throw up. I held my breath, waiting to see what would happen.

"Kieran?" Miss Owen took a step towards him. "Kieran? Are you okay?" She reached her arm out to him, but he jerked back as if he'd been burned, almost falling over his chair.

"They never should have sent him away from his mum," he blurted out. "They never should have separated them."

Everyone was staring at him. It was horrible, like watching a trapped animal.

"That's a very interesting point," said Miss Owen, as if it was perfectly normal for Kieran to be contributing to a class discussion. "Is there anything else you'd like to add?"

But Kieran's face had closed up again, as if someone

had drawn a heavy curtain across it. "This lesson is for losers," he said, picking up his copy of *Holes* and chucking it across the room. "No offence, yeah, but I'm outta here." He grabbed his bag, kicked his chair out of the way, and stumbled towards the door.

Miss Owen just stood there with her mouth open, as if she wasn't sure what to do next.

"Shame it's not really like *Holes*," whispered Gemma. "She'd be able to send him straight to Camp Green Lake and get rid of him for good."

9
A Day Out with Dad

When Charlie was born he had to stay in the special baby unit until he was three months old. Even then, when he was allowed home, he was so small and fragile Mum would stay awake half the night to make sure he was still breathing. He had this special alarm fitted to his chest which would ring if his heart stopped, and every time it went off, an ambulance would come and either Mum or Dad would go with him to the hospital.

One time, around ten months after he came home, Mum went to stay at my Aunty Hat's for the night. It was Aunty Hat's birthday and Mum was desperate for a break. The alarm hadn't gone off for ages and Charlie was getting stronger every day – but it went off that night, almost as if he knew Mum wasn't there.

I didn't actually hear the alarm or anything, I was in a different room fast asleep, but suddenly Dad was shaking me awake, pulling my coat on over my pyjamas, fumbling with the buttons. He bundled me into the back of the ambulance and it sped off towards the hospital, lights flashing, sirens blaring.

They put a mask over Charlie's face and then stuck a needle in his hand so they could hook him up to this massive machine with all these wires coming out of it. He didn't cry or anything, I think he was unconscious. I was the one who cried, all the way there. I screamed my head off. I was scared and I wanted my purple ribbon.

I don't remember much about the actual hospital or anything that happened while we were there, except for this red plastic playhouse in the children's waiting area, a little girl with huge eyes and no hair, and Dad's face when he came to tell me Charlie had pulled through.

Dad says I don't actually remember that night at all, that I was too young. He says I only *think* I remember because I've heard them talking about it so often. But whether I *really* remember, or only *think* I remember, when Mum suddenly announced on Saturday morning that she was going to stay at Aunty Hat's because she needed a break, I started to worry straight away that something bad might happen while she was gone.

I tried asking her if we could all go together; turn it into a proper family trip. She was in her bedroom packing, literally throwing things into a bag as if she couldn't wait to get away.

"You know how much I love going to Aunty Hat's," I said. "So does Charlie. And I could always bring my homework with—"

Mum didn't even look up. "Come on, Mads," she said. "It wouldn't really be a break for me if we all went, would it?" She chucked in her make-up bag and hairbrush. "I mean it's not as if I go away very often."

"I know, I know. It's just that I've got this funny feeling in my tummy…"

"You'll be fine," she said firmly. "It's only one day and I've left food to heat up. I'll be back by teatime tomorrow."

She didn't get it. She didn't get how anxious I was feeling.

Charlie wasn't worried at all; he was just happy to have Dad to himself for the weekend. He got this idea in his head that they'd spend the whole of Saturday playing football in the garden, doing special drills and stuff, but it didn't work out like that.

Dad sat in the lounge for ages after Mum left, staring

into space, a cold cup of tea in his hand. It was weird, like he was with us but not really with us.

I started to think he might be ill he was so out of it, but when I actually asked him what was wrong he jumped up, muttering something about some important papers he had to look through, and disappeared upstairs. Charlie wasn't happy. He trailed around the house after Dad, whining about the football team and Mr Maddox and how unfair everything was.

The whining got louder and more insistent as the day dragged on but Dad hardly seemed to notice; it was as if he'd forgotten we were even in the house. He'd do something ordinary, like open the cupboard to get out a glass, and then stand there for ages with the glass in his hand as if someone had put him in a trance. I took Charlie out into the garden in the end, just to stop him whingeing, but neither of us enjoyed it very much.

It was just as bad at dinner. I heated up the pasta Bolognese Mum had left and served it with my own home-made garlic bread and loads of grated cheese on top, just how Dad likes it. But when we actually sat down to eat he didn't say a word about the food or the amount of trouble I'd gone to. He didn't even mention the garlic bread.

I spent most of the meal blinking back tears. The bread tasted like cardboard. I chewed and chewed but it was impossible to swallow. I gave up in the end and scraped the whole lot in the bin.

"I hope you're not on one of those silly diets, Maddie," said Dad, noticing at last, but then his phone rang and he scooted out of the room, closing the door behind him.

He seemed to be back to his usual jolly self at breakfast, cracking jokes, trying to make us laugh, but it was difficult to tell whether he was genuinely happy or if it was all a big act. He said he'd planned a special day out, just the three of us, and that we'd need comfy clothes, sun hats and lots of suncream.

The last thing I felt like was a day out, especially with Mum away. I'd hardly slept, tossing and turning for ages, and then when I did finally drop off I had one of my horrible dreams. It was the one where Dad has a stroke, and then Mum and then Charlie. They're all in hospital together, their beds lined up like in *Goldilocks and the Three Bears*: a big bed for Dad, a medium-sized one for Mum and a tiny, little one for Charlie.

I go from bed to bed trying to wake them up, trying to get them to talk to me, but it's as if they're made of stone. "*Wake up!*" I shout, getting frantic. "*Wake up! Wake up! Wake up!*" I keep shaking them and shouting, but deep inside a part of me knows they're never going to wake up again.

I tried telling Dad I was tired, that I just wanted to stay at home and wait for Mum to get back, but he insisted I'd love it when we got there.

"We're going to a beautiful lake where you can hire boats," he said as we set off in the car. "I went there once when I was a little boy with your nan and granddad." He glanced at Charlie in the mirror. "I hope you're feeling strong, mate. I won't be able to manage the oars without you."

Charlie stared out of the window, ignoring him. He was still in a sulk about the football. Dad couldn't win him over that easily.

We left the motorway and were soon driving down a winding country lane. It was a beautiful morning, really warm but not as unbearably hot as the past few weeks. Slowly the knots in my stomach began to unravel and melt away as we drove deeper and deeper into the countryside.

The lake was set in acres of parkland surrounded by a thick forest of trees. Dad parked the car and we made our way down a long overgrown path to the boat-hire company. The sun shone through the trees, bouncing off the water like sprinkles of gold.

It was brilliant on the lake, almost magical. Even Charlie cheered up. It took a while to get the hang of the boat but eventually we settled into it, with Dad rowing at the front, Charlie kind of rowing at the back, and me perched in the middle, sketching the other boats as we went along.

We rowed for about half an hour and then let the boat float to the side of the lake so Charlie could have a rest. His mood had changed completely. He talked non-stop, telling Dad about school and football and Mr Maddox, describing a brilliant goal he'd scored at playtime, and then going on to describe how he'd celebrated, sliding halfway across the pitch on his knees.

When our hire time was almost up, we rowed back and had lunch by the river – big cheese and ham rolls, followed by 99 Flake ice creams. Nan used to love 99 ice creams, especially the flake. Sometimes she'd ask the ice-cream man for an extra one, pretending it was for me or Charlie, and then eat it herself.

My tummy lurched suddenly at the thought of never seeing her again. It just seemed too long. How could someone you love so much be gone *for ever*? No more cuddles or special treats or days out together. I couldn't bring myself to eat my last bite of flake – the best bit that's all covered in ice cream.

"Can we go home?" I said quietly. "I don't feel very well and I want to see Mum. She promised she'd be back by teatime."

Dad must have caught something in my tone. "What's up, Mads? You were fine on the water. Let's see some of those lovely sketches you did…"

I knew he was trying to distract me, to cheer me up a bit, but the day had lost its sparkle. My tummy was in knots again. It was like being on red alert all the time, waiting for something terrible to happen. I pulled my knees up under my chin and wrapped my arms round my legs, trying to hold myself together.

We set off for home as soon as Charlie finished his ice cream. I began to feel a bit better in the car. Dad asked me about school and promised to help me with my history project when we got in.

"We'll do football practice first," he said, winking at Charlie in the mirror, "and then straight on to the English Civil War. I know all about that scallywag Charles and how he came to a sticky end!"

But then just as we turned into our road, his phone started to ring. It was Sharon. I saw her name flash up on the screen a second before Dad answered.

"Sorry, you two," he said pulling over. "Can you go and wait for me inside? I might be a little while, but I've got to take this, it's important."

"What do you mean? What about playing football?" said Charlie. "You promised!"

Dad held his finger up to his lips and waved us out of the car but Charlie shook his head and started to kick the back of his seat. "I'm not going in until you tell me when we're going to play football!"

"Come on, Charlie." I pulled my front-door key out of my bag, but he shook his head again and kicked even harder.

"I don't want to. I want to stay in here with Dad."

"Hang on a sec," said Dad into the phone. He swung round to face Charlie, furious. "What do you think you're playing at? I've got to speak to someone and you'll just have to wait! The world doesn't revolve around you, Charlie Wilkins!"

Charlie's lip started to wobble. Dad hardly ever gets properly cross with him.

"Well why do you keep saying you'll play with me and then changing your mind? You didn't play with me at all yesterday." He rammed his fists into his eyes, trying not to cry. "I'll never get picked for the school team at this rate, I'll never be good enough…"

Dad's face softened. "Listen to me, Charlie. I am going to play footie with you, I swear, just as soon as I've finished this one phone call."

"Do you promise?" sniffed Charlie.

"Cross my heart. I might have to pop out for a bit, but

there'll be loads of time when I get back. It won't be dark for hours yet."

Charlie stiffened next to me. "Pop out?" he demanded. "What do you mean, pop out?"

The car was too hot suddenly, the heat pressing down on me making it difficult to breathe. Why did Dad have to speak to Sharon right this minute? Why couldn't he play with Charlie first and then call her back later? And what about helping me with my homework?

"I'm just going for a walk," I mumbled and slipped out of the car before Charlie started to kick off again.

It was obvious Sharon was important to Dad, more important than spending time with us, but I had no idea why. We'd never even heard of her until two weeks ago. I hurried down Morley Avenue towards the cemetery, anxious to get away. My tummy was hurting again, like I'd eaten way too many 99 Flake ice creams.

It was cool and calm in the cemetery. I trailed over to my usual bench by Nan's grave, relieved to be away from Dad and Charlie. I didn't blame Charlie for making such a fuss. I envied him in a way. There was a part of me that felt like confronting Dad myself, kicking the back of the seat, forcing him to tell us the truth about Sharon. But what if he said something terrible, like he'd fallen in love with her, whoever she was? What if the truth was so awful it changed everything for ever?

I sat and watched as an elderly couple arranged flowers on a fairly new-looking gravestone. The woman was sniffing into a white hanky and every now and then the man patted her arm. I still hadn't asked Dad about the woman who left the note, whether he knew who she was. I'd been too distracted by everything else that was going on at home.

Just to the right of the couple I noticed another man stumbling towards a grave on the other side of the path. He was drinking out of a bottle, but I wasn't close enough to see what it was. He stopped by the grave, leaning over and muttering something, waving the bottle and swaying from side to side. I knew I should probably go but I couldn't move. He took a step back, almost losing his balance, and then raised his arm and smashed the bottle down onto the headstone.

It made a horrible noise and a few people turned to see what was going on. The man swung round suddenly. "What are you all shhhtaring at?" he yelled. His words were thick and slurred. "Get lost, the lorra you!" His eyes came to rest on me. "What'sss your problem?" he hissed. "What are you looking at?" I shrank back into the bench as he lurched towards me. "I said, *whasss your problem, girlie?*" He stumbled back, swearing, and then took another lurching step forward, but before his foot could even touch the ground I sprang up from the bench and flew out of the cemetery.

I kept running all the way back down Morley Avenue without looking back. I knew he wasn't following me but I only dared stop when I got to the top of our street. I bent over double, gasping for breath, my heart racing so fast it actually hurt. How could something so horrible happen in such a peaceful place? *My special place?*

I waited until I could breathe normally again and then walked the rest of the way home. Mum was outside on the pavement, her phone in her hand. "*Maddie!* Why on earth did you run off like that? Where *were* you? You didn't text or anything."

"I'm sorry," I said, rushing over. I was *so* relieved to see her even if she was cross. "I was at the cemetery. I must've lost track of time." I reached my arms out for a hug but Mum stepped back slightly and I dropped them back down.

"At the cemetery *again*?" she said. "You can't just go off like that. I was really worried!"

"I know, I know, I'm sorry, I wasn't thinking. Where's Dad? Has he gone out?"

She let out a long sigh. "He has, but he won't be late. Come on, it's nearly teatime and I've promised Charlie pasta and meatballs with that special sauce he loves so much."

We had an okay evening in the end. Charlie helped Mum do the meatballs while I made a start on my history project, but it was difficult to concentrate. My eyes kept straying to the hall, desperate for the sound of Dad's key in the door, wondering where he was and when he'd be home. He'd promised he'd be back in time to play football with Charlie and to help me with my homework, but his promises didn't seem to mean very much these days.

He didn't get back until really late in the end, but even after I heard him come in it was impossible to get to sleep. I couldn't stop thinking about the man in the cemetery, the way he'd smashed the bottle on that grave and then lurched towards me. I'd decided not to say anything to Mum. I didn't want her to stop me going there altogether.

It was still on my mind as I set off for school the next morning. I waited by the gate until I saw other people walking through and then hurried along the path, only slowing down as I passed the grave where it happened. I expected there to be broken glass everywhere but I couldn't see a single shard. I edged a bit closer, wondering if the man had cleared it up himself, or if someone from the church had done it.

It was a new grave; I could tell from the stone that it hadn't been there for long. Some of the graves in the cemetery are over five hundred years old, but this one was smooth and shiny with modern writing. It was the writing I noticed first.

SAMANTHA BLACK
BELOVED WIFE AND MOTHER
1974–2013
FOREVER IN OUR HEARTS

I didn't think anything of it at first, but just as I turned to leave I noticed something else. Piled up in the corner of the grave were five small stones, so small you could easily miss them, each stone balanced carefully, one on top of the other. And that's when I realized. The word BLACK practically jumped out and hit me. Samantha Black had to be Kieran's mum. This had to be *her* grave.

10

Samantha Black

I rushed out of the cemetery and up Banner Road, trying to work out what it could mean; trying to piece it all together. Was the drunk man Kieran's dad? I was almost certain Mum said Kieran's mum was called Samantha when we were talking the other day. Was that why she said she *used* to know her? Because she was dead? And was that why Kieran freaked out in English? Or was it was just a coincidence? The name and the man and the stones…

Gemma was waiting for me at our usual place, waving as I came up the road.

"How was your weekend?" she asked as we made our

way to our lockers. "Did you get your history done?"

I nodded, showing her my book. "I only did three pages. I was out with my dad all day on Sunday so I didn't have much time."

"It's looks great," she said, glancing at my project. "Hey, Maddie, you'll never guess what happened yesterday. I was up at the shops with my mum and I saw *Nathan.*"

"What, Nathan from rounders?"

She nodded, blushing. "I didn't say hello or anything, I only saw him from a distance. By the way, promise you won't laugh when you see me tomorrow…"

"What do you mean? Why would I laugh?" I had no idea what she was on about but it had to be something to do with Nathan. It was so obvious she liked him.

"I can't tell you, Maddie. Just promise, okay?"

"Okay, I promise."

I hung around by my locker for another few minutes. I was late for nurture group but I felt a bit nervous about seeing Kieran. He was already there by the time I plucked up the courage to go in, so was Sally-Ann. I sat in my usual place and Vivian leaned across the table to hand me the pad. She was wearing a bright-yellow dress, her hair tied back with an orange scarf with tiny yellow butterflies printed all over it.

"I was supposed to be at the hospital this morning,"

Sally-Ann was saying, "but the appointment was cancelled at the last minute. I hate it when that happens."

"Yes it must be frustrating," said Vivian.

I glanced across at Kieran. He had his stones out but he wasn't doing anything with them, they were just sitting on the table in front of him. They were almost identical to the stones on the grave.

"It's not just frustrating," said Sally-Ann. "It feels like they don't think I'm ill enough to need the appointment."

"So going to the hospital makes you feel as if they're taking your illness seriously?"

Sally-Ann nodded. "When I don't go, I get more and more worried and the pain in my side gets much worse. Not that my mum ever notices, she couldn't care less. I was ill all weekend. Seriously, Vivian, it was a nightmare."

I doodled the word NIGHTMARE in bubble writing and then began to shade the letters in. I wondered if it was really such a nightmare or if, in a funny sort of way, Sally-Ann enjoyed the attention.

"Being ill can really spoil things," said Vivian. "How about you, Maddie, did you have a nice weekend?"

I nodded.

"Did you do anything special?"

"Um, I went out with my dad," I said, without really thinking. "We went to this lake and hired a rowing boat."

I started doodling again, my face on fire. It was the most I'd ever said in front of the others. The most I'd said at school for *months*.

Vivian gave me a big smile. "That sounds great," she said, "and it was such lovely weather. How about you, Kieran?"

"What?" He barely glanced up.

"Did you do anything special at the weekend?"

"*Um, I went out with my dad,*" he said, mimicking me in a really stupid high voice. "*We went to this lake and hired a rowing boat. We had such a great time, and it was* such *lovely weather!*"

Vivian put her head on one side as if she was taking him very seriously. "I wonder if hearing Maddie describe her day out with her dad made you think about how much you'd like to take a boat out yourself?"

He grabbed his stones and closed them tightly in his fist. "It didn't. I *hate* boats and I *hate* weekends."

There was an awkward silence after that. I carried on shading my bubble letters and Kieran started to balance his stones and then knock them down again. I kept glancing up at him, thinking about Samantha Black's grave and the man smashing the bottle, wondering if it really was his dad. Maybe that was why he hated weekends so much.

114

"Weekends can be difficult," said Vivian, just as the silence was beginning to feel really uncomfortable. "Especially if—"

"Oh, I've got the worst pain," said Sally-Ann suddenly, interrupting her. She grabbed her side, moaning. "It's really bad, right here…"

"Just take a few deep breaths," said Vivian calmly.

Sally-Ann tried to breathe in a couple of times but it only seemed to make things worse. "It's no good," she cried, her voice high and panicky. "I can't breathe; I can't take a proper breath. I need to get out of here. You'll have to call my mum! You'll have to tell her I'm not well!"

She scraped her chair back and stumbled towards the door.

"I'll just be a moment," said Vivian to me and Kieran. "Wait for me here."

She helped Sally-Ann out of the room and closed the door behind her.

"What are you drawing?" said Kieran as soon as she'd gone. "You and Daddy on the lake? You and Daddy having a lovely day out?"

He made it sound as if I was two years old and going out with my dad was the most babyish thing a person could do. I coloured in the "T" on NIGHTMARE. *This* was a nightmare – being stuck in a room with Kieran Black.

"Make sure you put a nice sun in the sky," he went on. "It was *such* lovely weather yesterday, remember?"

I stopped colouring and looked up. I think Vivian was right. Something about me saying I'd gone out with my dad had really got to him. He was using the same mocking voice he always used, but he was leaning forward, his fists clenched on the table, his eyes blazing with pent-up anger.

"I wasn't out on some perfect day with my dad if you must know," I said, getting angry myself. "We were only at the lake for a token treat! He doesn't even know I exist at the moment!"

He stared down at his stones. It was impossible to know what he was thinking. It was probably the most he'd ever heard me say.

"And my nan's buried in Banner Road Cemetery," I blurted out, before I could stop myself. "Just by the big weeping willow."

His head snapped up.

"So?"

I didn't know what to say then. My heart began to thump in my chest. I couldn't believe I'd stood up for myself, spoken to him like that, spoken *at all*. No one ever stands up to Kieran Black. I tried to think of some way to explain – something about Nan – but my mind had gone completely blank.

Just at that moment Vivian came back in. "Poor Sally-Ann. I've taken her to the medical room."

"W…was she okay?" I said, relieved to see her.

"Oh, I'm sure she'll be fine. Anyway, I'm afraid we're going to have to finish for today, but I'll see you both on Thursday."

Kieran got up and walked out without saying a word.

"I get in a panic sometimes, like Sally-Ann," I said to Vivian when he'd gone. "It's like there's this bird trapped in my chest, beating its wings really fast and I get this lump in my throat, sort of blocking it up so I can't get the words out…" I hesitated for a moment. It was the first time I'd confided in Vivian. The first time I'd told her how I was actually *feeling*. Maybe standing up to Kieran had given me that extra bit of courage I needed.

She smiled, encouraging me to carry on. I wiped my palms on my skirt. "It's just, well, it's just my mum keeps telling me how unhealthy it is for me to bottle things up, as if I'm *choosing* to be like that, but I can't help it, especially when I'm talking to her…"

"How do you mean?" said Vivian.

I shrugged. "I'm not sure. I…I…want to talk to her more but she's so worried about my little brother Charlie, I think she just expects me to be okay."

"What's the matter with your brother? Is there a particular reason she's so worried?"

"Um…he was born very premature – nearly three months early. He was so small they didn't think he'd survive the first night and then even when he came home he was still really ill and…" I took a breath, the words tumbling out now I'd started. "…and it was scary. He's okay now except his legs are still quite weak and it makes him walk funny, sort of clumsy, like his knees go in and his feet go out."

Vivian considered this for a moment. "That must've been a very anxious time for all of you, especially for you, Maddie. You must've wondered what happened to your safe little world – what happened to the mum you had *before* Charlie was born."

Tears pricked my eyes. I got why Charlie needed extra care and attention but it was still difficult sometimes. It still felt as if Mum loved him more than she loved me. Maybe that was the real reason I missed my nan so much. I never felt second-best with her.

Vivian reached out to touch my arm. "I was just wondering, Maddie, if those panicky feelings are hiding other feelings you find too painful to think about."

"What, you mean feelings about my mum?"

"Maybe, I don't know. We can talk about it more on

Thursday if you like, but you'd better get going now, you don't want to be late for your next class."

I'd almost forgotten about Kieran but he was waiting for me as I came out of the Blue Room. He yanked me away from the door and down the corridor, pulling me round to face him. "Why did you say that, about your nan's grave?" he said, blocking my way.

"N...n...no reason," I stammered. "Let me past."

He shook his head. "Not until you tell me."

I opened my mouth and closed it again, the words trapped in my throat.

Kieran tightened his grip on my arm. "Come on. You wouldn't have said it for nothing..."

"It's just there was a man there and he, he...smashed a bottle. I think he was drunk. That's all. N...n...now let me go or I'll be late."

I pushed against him, but he didn't budge. The bird was back, beating its wings so hard it hurt. He was such a bully. I didn't care if it was his mum who was buried in the cemetery; I just wanted him to leave me alone. I couldn't believe I'd actually started to feel sorry for him.

"I mean it, Kieran, let me go!"

I thought he was going to hit me for a minute, he looked so angry, but then suddenly he started to blink really fast.

"Just don't tell anyone about the drunk man," he hissed.

Our faces were so close they were almost touching.

"Okay! I won't...I...I...wouldn't!"

He stepped to the side and I stumbled past him and down the corridor, too scared to look round in case he was following. The man *had* to be his dad. *He had to be*. Why else would he say that? Why would he care?

11
Hit-and-Run

Somehow I managed to avoid Kieran for the rest of the day but I was still feeling shaky when I got to art. I kept remembering the way he'd pushed his face into mine, threatening me not to tell anyone. It was too late to unsay what I'd said – he knew I'd seen the man smash the bottle.

I was supposed to be working on my portrait of Gemma – I'd finished her hair and just made a start on her eyes – but I couldn't stop thinking of Kieran's eyes, furious one minute, blinking back tears the next.

"Hey, did you see Mrs Turner's baby?" said Gemma, nudging me to get my attention. "She brought her in to show everyone during registration. She was so cute; she had this big pink bow in her hair."

I shook my head.

Mrs Turner is one of the school secretaries – the friendly one who doesn't mind how many times you lose something or forget to return letters and permission slips.

"I wish you'd seen her, Mads. I put my finger in the pram and she grabbed hold of it. I couldn't believe how strong her little fingers were. I...I..." She turned away suddenly as if she didn't want me to see her face.

"What's the matter?"

"Nothing!"

"Come on, Gem. What's wrong?"

She reached down to get a tissue out of her bag, still hiding her face from me.

"Nothing, I'm fine," she said, but I could tell she was crying from her voice.

"Is it something to do with Mrs Turner's baby? Why are you so upset?"

Just then Mrs Morris came over to look at our portraits. Gemma scraped her chair back and sprang up.

"I'm sorry but I'm not feeling very well," she muttered. "Can I go and get some fresh air?"

She grabbed her bag and ran out without waiting for an answer.

"That's not like Gemma," said Mrs Morris. "Is she okay?"

I shrugged, wondering what was going on. "I'm not sure. I think she was upset about something but she wouldn't tell me…"

Gemma didn't come back for the rest of the lesson. I figured she must've gone home. I tried texting her after school but she didn't text back. I didn't see Kieran either. I was worried he might be waiting for me outside school, that he might follow me down Banner Road and threaten me again. I hung around in the playground for ages, frightened to leave, wishing Gemma was with me, but there was no sign of him.

I decided to ask Mum about it later. I was sitting in the kitchen, struggling through my French homework while she got dinner ready – some sort of weird salad with pears, cheese and walnuts. I didn't have a clue how much she'd tell me about Kieran's family, but I was convinced she must know something.

"Mum, you know the nurture group?" I said as casually as I could. "Well, I know I said I wasn't going back, but I did in the end. I've already had two more sessions…"

Mum glanced up. "Yes I know. I spoke to Mrs Palmer this morning…"

"Oh, right. You didn't say…"

"I'm not checking up on you, Maddie. I was just worried.

How are you getting on anyway?"

"Okay, I suppose. I like Vivian, she's really nice. So do you remember I told you about a boy called Kieran Black? How he's in the group too…"

"Hmmm?"

"Well, his mum isn't *dead*, is she?"

Mum looked up again.

"It's just…I was walking through the cemetery this morning and I noticed there was a grave near to Nan's grave with the name *Samantha Black* written across it, and I remembered that you said you *used* to know his mum…"

"Listen, Maddie, I wasn't joking when I said you were spending too much time at the cemetery…"

"What's that got to do with anything?" I said, frustrated. Why did she have to keep going on about the cemetery? "I just want to know about Kieran's mum."

"Has Kieran talked about her in the nurture group?"

"No, not really…I was just wondering…" I trailed off, not sure what else I could say. I didn't want to mention the stones or the drunk man.

Mum carried on slicing the pears as if she was deciding what to say next. She's always so careful if it's got anything to do with work.

"It is his mum's grave, Mads," she said after a bit. "She died nearly two years ago in an accident. It was a hit-and-run, late at night. It was in the paper. They never caught the person who did it."

"Oh, that's so sad!"

Mum nodded. "I know; it was awful. I didn't know her that well, we weren't close friends or anything, but I knew who she was…"

"Is that why his dad goes to the clinic? Did her death make him start drinking?"

"Is that what Kieran's told you?"

I shook my head. "He hardly says anything in the group. It was you who told me. Well, you said something about working with his family. I thought you meant his mum but now…"

"Come on, Maddie," she cut in. "You know I never talk about my patients at the clinic. Kieran's been through a really tough time, and I'm sure things are still difficult for him, but I'm not going to discuss his dad with you so please don't ask me again, okay?"

I shrugged, dying to know more.

"I mean it, Maddie. Not another word. Now can you please get Charlie in from the garden? It's time to eat and he's been out there for ages."

Charlie was on the patio, right in the middle of a full-blown commentary.

"…what a pass and now it's Charlie Wilkins on the ball.

He's got real talent, this guy. He runs with it, past one, past two, Wilkins is still going. Unbelievable – the strength in this boy's legs! The ball is literally glued to his feet. Great skill! Only the keeper to beat now. He shoots! He scooooores! It's Wilkiiiiiiiiins! Charlie Wilkins wins the game!"

He turned and ran across the grass, sliding onto his knees in celebration. It was nice to see him score the winning goal, even if he was the only one on the team.

"It's time to come in," I said when he'd finished. "And wait until you see what's for dinner!"

I lay awake for ages that night but not because of bad dreams or listening out for Dad. I couldn't stop thinking about Kieran. Someone had killed his mum. Run her over and then left her there to die. It was too terrible to imagine. Who was looking after him? Who was making sure he was okay? I wondered if he'd gone to the cemetery late last night or early this morning to clear up the broken glass, if that was when he'd left the small pile of stones.

I remembered what he said in English that day, about how wrong it was to separate Stanley from his mum when they sent him to Camp Green Lake.

Kieran had been separated from his mum for ever.

12

Asking for Help

It was boiling hot the next morning. Dad said it was forecast to be the hottest day of the year so far. I trailed through the cemetery on my way to school, slowing down by Samantha Black's grave. It felt weird knowing it was Kieran's mum buried there, to have discovered something so private about him.

Gemma was waiting for me at our usual place. The second I saw her I realized what she'd been talking about when she told me not to laugh. I couldn't believe it. She'd had her hair cut much shorter, right up to her shoulders, with loads of feathery layers.

"What's happened to your plaits?" I cried, rushing up

look like you've been on one of those make-
grammes!"

What do you think?" she said, twirling round. "I had
to literally beg my mum. We went to this really trendy
hairdresser on the High Street; they do a special price on
Mondays. It was so much fun. They brought me a drink
in a cocktail glass with one of those little umbrellas and
then spent ages talking to me about what style I wanted
before they actually cut it…"

"But I thought you were *ill* yesterday? I thought that's
why you went home during art? You were really upset."

She shook her head, her smile slipping for a moment.
"No I was fine, it was nothing. So do you think it suits me,
Maddie? Come on, be honest…"

"It really suits you," I said slowly, still a bit confused.
"Seriously, you look so much older. Are you wearing
mascara?"

"Yes and lipgloss, but it doesn't show that much, does
it? I don't want to get into trouble. I sneaked out the
house while my mum and dad were still asleep!"

"Um, it does show a bit, but keep your head down and
you might get away with it."

I kept expecting her to show me her maths homework
or our latest English assignment but she only wanted to
talk about her hair and her make-up and how much she

was looking forward to rounders club – as if they'd cut off her old personality along with her plaits. I couldn't help sneaking glances at her as we walked down the corridor, an uneasy feeling lodging itself in my stomach. It wasn't just the new haircut, or the way she kept going on about Nathan. She was hiding something from me, I was sure of it.

There was no sign of Kieran at registration. I found myself watching the door, waiting for him to burst in and disrupt everything. It was probably stupid, but I couldn't help worrying that something had happened to him, especially if the drunk man really was his dad. A few weeks ago I would've been thrilled at the thought of a Kieran-free day, but that was before I knew what he was actually going through.

He didn't turn up for the rest of that day, or the day after. They're really strict about attendance at Church Vale – Mrs Palmer's always going on about the direct relationship between attendance and future achievement – but I could hardly remember the last time Kieran had been at school for a full *day* let alone a full week.

It was unbearably hot at rounders on Wednesday; like being baked alive. Gemma's make-up was smudged round her eyes like a panda and her hair had wilted. Nathan was captain of our team and he seemed to be taking it very seriously, giving us loads of advice while we were waiting to bat.

"I'm going to make such a fool of myself," Gemma muttered when he'd finished his pep talk. "I can't even remember if you're supposed to drop the bat or take it with you..."

"Drop it," I said. "Just keep your eye on the ball and you'll be fine."

But when she got up to bat she missed by a mile and then threw the bat up in the air, squeaking like a mouse.

"Run!" I shouted. "Just run!" But it was too late, the backdrop threw the ball to first base and she was out.

"Come on, Maddie," said Mr Skinner as I got up for my turn. "You did really well last week. I know it's hot, but your team's counting on you!"

My legs began to feel a bit wobbly when he said that, like he was putting too much pressure on me. I peered across the field, wondering if Nan was there, if she was going to help me again. It was difficult to see anything through the shimmering haze of heat, but I kept my eyes fixed on the exact same spot I'd seen her last time and the same warm feeling filled my belly.

A boy called Scott was bowling. He drew the ball back, swinging his arm round and round as if he was playing baseball.

"Hey, unfair tactics!" Nathan called out. "You're not allowed to do that in rounders!"

"Just bowl the ball, Scott," said Mr Skinner. "There's no need for tricks, thank you very much!"

Scott did one more roll and then let go. The ball flew towards me like a bullet. I concentrated as hard as I could on the thought of Nan standing by the sycamore trees, watching me, making sure I was okay, as I swung my bat and whacked it way over Scott's head and into the field.

"Run!" shouted Nathan as I took off towards first base. The rest of the team cheered me on: "Mad-die! Mad-die!"

I made it all the way round to third before Scott got the ball back. I was still one base away from scoring my first rounder but it was the greatest feeling in the world. I'd had no idea I'd enjoy rounders club so much when Gemma dragged me along.

"Why can't I be as good as you?" Gemma moaned when I flopped back down on the grass next to her.

"I'm not *that* good," I said, glancing back at the sycamore trees, knowing I'd only managed to hit it so far with Nan's help. "And anyway, you only missed because of Nathan."

The words shot out before I could stop them.

"What do you mean?" she said, turning scarlet.

"Nothing...I didn't mean anything, it's just I thought

maybe you kept missing because you like him and…"

"I don't!" she cried. "I don't like him!" She put her hands up to her flaming cheeks. "Well okay, I *do* a bit. Actually I like him a lot, Maddie, like LOADS…but he's never going to notice someone like me, not in a million years."

"He *might* notice you," I said. "Especially if you managed to hit the ball!"

She somehow blushed even more. "I'll *never* be able to hit the ball," she groaned. "I can't even *see* it without my glasses on, but they make me look like such a geek."

"Are you being serious? Is that why you keep taking them off? And there was me thinking you only did it in case they got broken!"

We were still laughing about it on the way home. Gemma said she'd had no idea where the ball was, or if Scott had even bowled it yet. "I just randomly swung the bat and hoped for the best. I mean if the ball was a bit bigger I might've stood a decent chance."

"Well I can't see Mr Skinner changing the size of the balls any time soon, so I think your best bet is to wear your glasses. They look nice anyway, they really suit you, and think how surprised Nathan would be if you actually managed to hit the ball. You might even score a rounder for the team."

I couldn't believe how easy it was for us to talk about Nathan. In fact I couldn't believe how easy it was to talk full stop. It was the closest I'd felt to her in ages. Maybe opening up to Vivian was helping me more than I realized? I was tempted to tell Gemma about the sessions and how anxious I'd been feeling since Nan died, but the truth was that I was a tiny bit frightened she wouldn't understand; that she might think it was weird that I needed special help from a counsellor.

When I walked into the Blue Room the next morning Kieran was already there, sitting in my seat. I stood by the door for a moment, relieved to see him in a way, but uncomfortable about being forced to sit somewhere different. I grabbed the pad from Vivian and sat as far away from him as I could.

"Sally-Ann won't be joining us this morning," said Vivian. "It's just the three of us."

"Don't tell me," said Kieran, sneering. "She's discovered some new allergy. Haven't you realized yet, there's nothing wrong with her, she just pretends to be ill to get attention."

Vivian kept her eyes fixed on his face. She has this amazing way of listening as if she's thinking things through very carefully. "Well, Sally-Ann isn't here to defend herself, so it wouldn't be right to discuss her allergies. However, it's probably true that we all have

133

certain strategies for getting attention. The way I see it, drawing attention to yourself, however you choose to do it, is nothing to be ashamed of. It's just a way of asking for help."

"That's rubbish," said Kieran. "The last thing I want is anyone helping me." He shot me a look. "I don't want any help and I don't need it."

"How about you, Maddie?" said Vivian. "What do you think?"

I shrugged, staring down at my pad. I could feel Kieran's eyes on me, accusing me. Letting me know he wanted me to butt out. It was hot and stuffy; sweat dripped down my back.

"Sometimes," Vivian went on, "not saying anything is still saying something. It can still be a way of asking for help."

My tummy tightened. She was talking about me. I tried to work out what she meant – if keeping everything bottled up inside was just my way of showing her and Mrs Palmer and Mum how scared and out of control I'd been feeling. I drew a big mouth on my pad and then scribbled over it until it was completely covered.

"So basically," said Kieran, still sneering, "if you're noisy it's a cry for help, if you're quiet it's a cry for help and if you pretend to be ill it's a cry for help. Is *everything*

134

a cry for help? How about laughing too much? Or crying? Or stuffing your face? Or starving yourself?"

"Pretty much all of those, yes," said Vivian. "But it sounds to me as if you're saying that any way of asking for help is rubbish."

Kieran narrowed his eyes. "Well I'm not about to ask you for any help, if that's what you mean."

Vivian shook her head. "No, that's not what I mean exactly. I mean that sometimes it's very difficult to ask for help and that accepting it is even harder. *If everything Vivian says is rubbish then I don't have to think about it, or do anything with it, I can just throw it all in the bin.*"

I held my breath watching Kieran's face. He looked as if he wanted to put *Vivian* in the bin.

But he just took his stones out and started piling them up and knocking them down. I wondered if they helped him to calm down when he was upset, like me sleeping with my ribbon.

"So if I think everything you say is rubbish," he said after a bit, "why do I bother coming here in the first place?"

"Only you know the answer to that," said Vivian. "Maybe there's a part of you that does want some help, however scary that might seem."

Kieran didn't say anything this time, and Vivian's

words hung in the air. I think she was trying to say that we were being brave just by turning up to nurture group.

"It's time to finish now," she said a few moments later. "Thank you for coming. I'll see you both on Monday."

"You'll be lucky," muttered Kieran, grabbing his stones and scraping his chair back so hard it fell on the floor. "And in case you were wondering, the only reason I come here is because Mrs Palmer makes me."

He left his chair where it was and strode out. I waited for a moment and then walked around the table to pick it up and tuck it back under the table.

"Thank you, Maddie. You didn't need to do that, but I appreciate it. Things can get a bit heated in here sometimes."

"It's okay, I'm not scared of Kieran," I said, and I meant it. I used to be scared of him, but I wasn't any more, not now I knew about his mum.

I was just about to hand the pad back, to tell Vivian how much the sessions were helping me, even if I still found it difficult to talk about my feelings, when something caught my eye through the open door.

It was a flash of blue.

A flash of blue silk.

I blinked and then looked again, wondering if my eyes were playing tricks on me. Someone wearing a blue silk headscarf had just walked straight past the room and down the corridor.

13
Another Change

I rushed out into the corridor. It was her, the woman from the cemetery. I could see her up ahead. She was smaller than I remembered and impossibly thin, but it was definitely her. I opened my mouth to say something but nothing came out. It was as if someone had stolen my voice again, like the day Nan collapsed. *Wait!* I thought. *Don't go. Please don't go. I really need to talk to you.*

She disappeared round the corner heading towards the exit.

"Wait," I tried again, and this time it came out – not very loud, but loud enough to spur me on.

I rushed down the corridor and round the corner,

pushing past anyone who got in my way, but she wasn't there. I swallowed down a sob, batting the tears away. She couldn't have disappeared that quickly. *She couldn't!* She must've gone into the school office.

I waited for as long as I dared, praying she'd come out. I had to speak to her but I couldn't go barging in without a good reason. I should've moved faster, called out louder. The hall began to clear around me until it was almost empty. A monitor came over to ask where I was supposed to be, threatening to report me if I didn't go straight to class.

It was a nightmare. I couldn't stop thinking about her for the rest of the morning. I kept imagining a flash of blue silk every time I came out of class or turned the corner. I needed to know who she was and how she knew Nan and what she was doing here, at Church Vale. It was so frustrating. But there was no way of finding out. I didn't even know her name.

"What's going on with you and Kieran Black?" said Gemma. We were in the canteen at lunch and she was staring past my shoulder across the room. "He hasn't taken his eyes off you for a single second, not for the entire time we've been in here."

"There's nothing going on," I said, thinking of the nurture group and how he'd kicked off, the way he'd looked at me when he said he didn't need any help. "I'm not even turning round." He was only trying to intimidate me, scare me into keeping quiet, but I meant it when I said to Vivian that I wasn't scared any more. I felt sorry for him more than anything else.

He kicked off again later that day during art. Mrs Morris had displayed all our portraits around the studio for everyone to see, like a mini exhibition. They weren't finished yet, but she thought it would be cool for us to see how they were progressing so far. There was a buzz in the room as we walked round, everyone talking about which ones they liked best and who they could recognize.

Kieran turned up fifteen minutes late. By that time everyone had claimed their pictures so his was the only one left, propped up on a table against the wall. He'd done a simple portrait of a woman using very thin charcoal. I thought it was really beautiful, especially the eyes, and I wondered if it was supposed to be his mum.

A shadow passed across his face as he scanned the room and saw the picture on show. I remembered the way he'd been working on it, bent right over the paper so no one else could see what he was doing. A split second later he lunged towards the table, grabbed the portrait and tore it in half – chucking the two torn pieces at Mrs Morris.

It all happened so fast Mrs Morris didn't have time to say anything or try to stop him as he stormed out of the room – she seemed to be as shocked as the rest of us. She asked us to get on with our work and then spent ages taping the two pieces of the portrait back together until it was difficult to see it had been torn in half in the first place.

At the end of the lesson she asked me to stay back for a minute. I stood at the front waiting for the others to file out, wondering if I was in trouble. Was she going to say my marks had slipped or I wasn't concentrating enough in class?

"There's no need to look so scared, Maddie," she said when everyone had gone. "I just wanted to have a chat with you about your portrait of Gemma. You know, in all the years I've been doing portraits with Year Eight, yours is definitely the most unusual. I think it's fantastic."

I stared at her as if she was speaking another language. *My portrait? Fantastic?*

"Seriously, Maddie," she went on. "I can't wait until it's finished. I'm going to get it framed and put it up where everyone can see it. I just can't believe how well you've managed to capture the essence of Gemma's face using something as simple as newspaper."

I couldn't believe it either. Any of it. I was smiling so hard it felt as if my face was about to split in half.

"That was all really," she said. "I just wanted you to know how impressed I am and that I've told Mrs Palmer as well. You should be really proud."

I practically floated through the rest of the day. I couldn't wait to tell Mum and Dad; it was ages since I'd had anything good to say about school. I forgot all about Kieran kicking off and the woman in the blue headscarf, it was as if Mrs Morris's words had pushed everything else out of my head.

I rushed out of school and down Banner Road as soon as the bell rang; my tummy flipping over every time I replayed the conversation. *My portrait*, the best she'd ever seen! I could feel the words fizzing around inside me, warm and bubbly, bursting to get out. I didn't even stop at the cemetery, there was no time. I wanted to get straight home.

I'd only been in for about half an hour when Mum and Charlie got back. They came slamming through the front door shouting at each other about something. Charlie yelled at Mum to leave him alone and then ran straight into the garden and began to kick the ball, pounding it against the wall.

"What's going on?" I asked, as Mum came in behind him. "I don't think the wall can take much more!"

"I don't think *I* can take much more," said Mum. "There's been an *incident* at school."

"What do you mean, an *incident*? What happened?"

"I'm not sure exactly. Mr Maddox was waiting for me when I went to pick him up. He said Charlie lost his temper, kicked a boy in the year below him called Finn. We had to go and talk to Mrs Conner. It sounded really bad."

"What did you say? Did you tell them how upset he's been about the football team?"

Mum shook her head. "I don't want Charlie to get into the team just because they feel sorry for him. He'd *hate* that, and anyway, *kicking* someone, Maddie. He can't do that however angry he gets..." She glanced out of the window to where he was kicking the ball. "I don't know, maybe we've given in to him too much, treated him differently? It's just I can't bear to see him get hurt..."

Charlie...it was *always* about Charlie. I looked past Mum's worried face, my eyes blurring, desperate to conjure up Nan behind the kitchen counter – desperate to go back to the days when she was waiting for me after school, excited to hear my news.

"*Mrs Morris loves my portrait of Gemma,*" I whispered. "*She thinks it's fantastic...*"

And suddenly Nan was there, lifting her arms above her head, cheering for me just like she used to whenever I had something exciting to tell her. She was even less smudgy than on the rounders field, more solid. I could almost stretch my hand out and touch her…

"Maddie? *Maddie?*" Mum touched my arm. "What's the matter? Why are you crying?"

I blinked at her, confused for a moment and when I looked back there was nothing there, no outline or anything, just thin air.

"Maddie? *Please*, talk to me." Mum pulled me into her arms. "What is it? What's happened?"

"I just miss my nan," I said, leaning my face against her shoulder. It felt as if someone was squeezing my heart, wringing it out, as if the tears would never stop. Mum held me tight, stroking my hair, telling me over and over that everything was going to be okay, and I wanted to believe her, more than anything, but I knew it wasn't true. Nan would never be there again. She'd never be waiting for me in the kitchen after school to hear my news.

Dad was hardly around all weekend. He had a big rewiring job on Saturday and then on Sunday he left straight after breakfast without really saying much. Mum said he had an arrangement he couldn't break and that there was nothing he could do. I wanted to ask her straight out if he was spending the day with Sharon, but every time I opened my mouth I had a rush of nerves and clamped it shut again; scared Mum might say something I didn't want to hear.

Charlie was much more vocal than me. Dad usually takes him to the park on Sunday mornings to play football with some other dads and their children and it was the third week in a row he'd missed it. He was in the foulest mood all day, slamming in and out of the house, refusing to come in for lunch, answering Mum back.

Dad didn't get home until just after eleven in the end. I was still awake, listening out for him, my ribbon twisted round my hand so tight it hurt. As soon as I heard his key in the door I let out a long, ragged breath, but a moment later Mum was in the hall, half-shouting, half-hissing at him for being so late.

I sat up, straining to hear what she was saying… something about putting us second and getting his loyalties wrong.

"I knew this would happen," she said, her voice growing louder. "You don't know what sort of day I've had. It's so bloody selfish. Leaving me here to pick up the pieces! It's up to you to talk to the kids. I can't keep fobbing them off. It's Charlie's check-up next week and I'm already worried enough about that!"

I couldn't hear what Dad said back, if he said anything, but Mum went on and on. He was letting us down, putting himself first, forgetting his responsibilities, upsetting everyone. It was horrible. She was still hurling insults at him when Charlie pushed my door open.

"Do something, Maddie," he said. "Please, I don't like it. Make them stop."

I pulled my covers back. "Come on, you can sleep in here with me if you don't mind squashing up."

He stumbled over in the dark and climbed in. "I hate it when Mum gets angry with Dad. It sounds like she hates him, like they'll never make up."

"I'm sure it sounds worse than it is," I said, wrapping my arms round him, holding him close. "Don't you remember what Nan used to say whenever Mum was cross?"

He shook his head, snuggling closer, his body hot and sticky through his T-shirt.

"You *must* remember. She used to say, *Calm down, Sophie. There's no point getting your kippers in a twist.*"

"It's not *kippers*, Maddie, it's knickers."

"Well, some people say knickers, but not Nan. She always said kippers."

"Don't get your kippers in a twist," Charlie said sleepily. "That's funny." He lay very still for a bit. I thought he'd dropped off to sleep, but then he said, "I'm not sorry I hurt Finn the other day. Mrs Conner made me apologize but I had my fingers crossed behind my back so it doesn't count."

"Why did you kick him in the first place?"

His whole body tensed up. "He's an idiot. He called me a spaz and said I was a midget."

One or two kids at school have teased Charlie about his size before, and about the way he walks, but it's never really bothered him. I had no idea who Finn was, but I felt like kicking him myself.

"Did you tell Mrs Conner?"

Charlie shook his head against my chest. "There's no point. But if Finn says anything else, I'll kick him again, or worse. I swear he'll be sorry he ever messed with me in the first place."

He was trying to big himself up, act the tough guy, but he'd probably never felt so small in his life.

"Hey, Charlie, who's the best footballer in the world?"

I could almost feel him rolling his eyes.

"Messi, obviously."

"And how tall is he?"

"Small," he said.

147

"You just remember that, next time Finn, or anyone else, calls you names."

I felt his body relax against mine and I pulled him even closer, holding him tight. A few moments later his breathing slowed and then a little while later he began to snore. It was like lying next to a tractor, or some kind of high-powered drill. I was still aware of Mum shouting, but her voice was muffled, as if it was coming from far away – muffled enough to pretend it was someone else's mum shouting at someone else's dad.

Charlie was still fast asleep and snoring when I woke up the next morning. I slipped out of bed and got dressed, anxious to see Dad, to make sure everything was okay. I was aching all over, as if I hadn't slept properly for weeks. I ran downstairs and was about to go in the kitchen when I realized Mum was already in there on the phone. I pressed my ear right up against the door, holding my breath so she wouldn't know I was listening.

"Oh, Hat, I just don't know how we're going to tell her," she was saying. I realized she was talking to my aunt. "You know how hard she's found it since her nan died and now *this*! It's all been so sudden – getting in touch with him like that, completely out of the blue, asking him to meet up…"

My legs felt wobbly, as if they weren't strong enough to take my weight. She was talking about Dad and Sharon, she had to be. I started to tremble all over.

"I really wish you were here, Hat," said Mum, her voice breaking. "I wish I knew how to handle this but I feel completely out of my depth… I know, I know, Charlie will be fine; I'm really not worried about him, for once. But I honestly don't think Maddie can cope with one more change."

I turned and raced back upstairs, reaching around Charlie's head and under my pillow for my ribbon. What did she mean? What was going on? What were they going to tell me? I held the ribbon up to my face, breathing in the satiny smell, trying to stop the awful churning in my stomach. Were Mum and Dad breaking up? Was Dad leaving us for Sharon? Is that what she was talking about? Was that the change?

The floor shifted beneath my feet – I could actually feel it move, as if an earthquake was happening right there in my room. I grabbed hold of my headboard, trying to steady myself. I was breathing too fast, short gasping breaths as the panic began to spiral out of control.

And then I did something I'd never done before, not even when Nan died. I unwrapped the ribbon from round my hand and slipped it into my bag.

149

14
Opening Up

I could see Gemma waiting for me in the distance as I came up Banner Road, but I couldn't face her, I was too upset. I didn't know what to say anyway. I crossed the road to the other side and slipped in the side entrance. We're not supposed to go in that way unless we have an early-morning job, like setting up for assembly, but it was easy enough to pretend I was with the other monitors.

Mum had still been talking to Aunty Hat when I'd come back down to leave for school. She mouthed something about breakfast, as if I was really going to sit down with her and have a slice of toast or a bowl of cereal. I couldn't imagine ever eating breakfast again, not in a normal way, all of us sitting round the table together, not if Dad was leaving us to live with Sharon.

I hid in the girls' toilet until registration, locking myself in a cubicle, my ribbon wrapped round my hand like a bandage. I felt massively guilty about bringing it to school, as if I'd broken some unspoken rule. Mum would go mad if she found out, but there was no way I could get through the day without it.

Kieran and Sally-Ann were already in the Blue Room when I got there. Sally-Ann was telling Vivian about her weekend, something to do with the hospital. She trailed off as I came in, holding her side and wincing as if she was in pain.

"Hello, Maddie," said Vivian. "Do you want the pad?"

I took it from her without saying anything and sat at the far end of the table. Most of the session passed in a blur. Sally-Ann carried on telling Vivian about the hospital; how she'd been tested for a new batch of allergies. She went on and on, listing all the allergies she might or might not have, until suddenly Kieran slammed his fist down on the table.

"Just shut up, can't you! Some people have serious illnesses, they even *die*! Who cares about whether you've got a stupid allergy to dust mites?"

"Well you can actually die from allergies too, if you

must know!" said Sally-Ann. She stuck her chin out but her face was bright red and she was blinking back tears.

Vivian waited a moment and then she said, "Sometimes it must feel as if nothing else is as serious as what we're going through ourselves."

"Hang on," said Kieran. "What are you saying? That an allergy to dust mites is as serious as someone dying?"

"No, of course not," said Vivian. "I'm just aware that Sally-Ann's allergies cause her a lot of anxiety, even though you might be going through something yourself that feels far more serious than that."

Kieran sat there fuming. He was obviously thinking about his mum, not that he'd ever tell Vivian. He took a single stone out of his pocket and rolled it round and round between the palms of his hands as if he was trying to smooth away all the rough edges.

"So are you going to say sorry then or what?" said Sally-Ann, still blinking. "Maybe you should engage your brain before you start mouthing off."

Kieran raised his eyes to look at her. "Why should I say sorry? Some things *are* more serious than a bunch of pathetic allergies. When you die it's for ever. You don't go to the hospital and have a few tests done or get a load of pills. You don't get *cured*. I mean are you too thick to understand or what?"

Sally-Ann opened her mouth and closed it again.

"Perhaps it would be helpful for you to talk about this some more, Kieran?" said Vivian. "To tell us why you're so angry."

"*Didn't you hear me?*" said Kieran, scraping his chair back and drawing himself up. "When someone dies it's *for ever*, so how is talking about it going to help?"

He didn't bother waiting for an answer; he kicked his chair halfway across the room and walked out, slamming the door behind him.

I had a sudden urge to run after him. To tell him I understood. That I was never going to see my nan again, that she was gone for ever. I needed my ribbon. I could almost feel it in my bag, my hands itching to reach for it, my breathing tight. Just one touch and I'd be able to cope.

"He's so obnoxious," said Sally-Ann, pushing her fringe out of her eyes. "It's like he thinks he's the only person who's ever suffered."

"Well I feel sorry for him," I blurted out, surprising myself. "My nan died over six months ago and I still miss her every single day."

"I'm sorry to hear about your nan, Maddie," said Vivian. "Were you very close?"

"Very," I said, staring down at the pad, a heavy feeling

pressing down on my chest like a brick. "She was more like a mum to me than a nan."

"Yeah, sorry about your nan," said Sally-Ann, "but Kieran didn't actually *say* his nan had died, or his granddad, or anyone else, did he? He just said *when* someone dies, as if he was trying to prove a point. He was just doing it to put me down."

I glanced at Vivian, wondering if she knew about Kieran's mum. How much had Mrs Palmer told her?

"Well I can't tell you what Kieran meant exactly," she said to Sally-Ann. "Perhaps he'll explain to you himself on Thursday." She glanced at her watch. "It's time for you to go to your first class now, girls, but thank you for coming."

Gemma was waiting for me by my locker.

"Why did you go in the side entrance?" she said. "Didn't you see me waving by the gates? One minute you were there and then you'd disappeared and I've got so much to tell you."

I stuck my head in my locker, pretending to be busy with my books. "I'm really sorry, I was dying for the loo and I couldn't wait. So what's the big news?"

"You'll never guess," she said, hopping from foot to foot. "I was in the newsagent's looking for a birthday card for my mum and Nathan came in to buy a Coke. I mean what are the chances of that? Two weekends in a row!

154

God, I hope he doesn't think I'm stalking him or anything…"

"What happened? Did you speak to him this time?"

She shook her head. "No, but I smiled and I think he smiled back. Look I'll show you exactly what he did and you tell me if you think it was a smile." She pulled me round to face her and attempted to smile, her face twisting up on one side. "Well?"

I couldn't help laughing, it was so funny. "I don't know," I said. "Are you sure he didn't have toothache or something?"

"What do you mean? It was definitely a smile." But she laughed as well, linking her arm through mine as we made our way down the corridor.

I tried to concentrate on what she was saying as she gabbled on about Nathan and rounders club and how she was definitely going to wear her glasses on Wednesday so she could see the ball. It was a relief to have something else to think about for a few minutes, but I knew I wouldn't be able to keep the anxiety about Mum and Dad rowing and the phone call to Aunty Hat squashed down for very long.

In English we had to discuss and then write about the holes that Stanley and the other boys at Camp Green Lake were made to dig every day as part of their punishment.

The camp is in the middle of a desert and the boys are forced to dig in the heat of the midday sun until they're literally collapsing with exhaustion.

I only managed to write a paragraph and when I read it through it didn't even make sense. Mum's words kept going round and round my head. *I honestly don't think Maddie can cope with one more change. I honestly don't think Maddie can cope with one more change.* Nan used to say I was better at coping than I gave myself credit for, but that was only because she was there to look after me, to cheer me on.

When we'd finished, Miss Owen asked us to think about the holes in Stanley's life *before* he came to the camp, how he didn't have any friends, for example. She said for homework she wanted us to write about a hole in our own lives. Either something really serious like a bereavement or moving country – or something we'd all experienced, like leaving our friends behind when we moved from primary school to secondary.

I turned round to look at Kieran, to see how he'd react, but he wasn't there. The place where he usually sat was empty.

"I have no idea what I'm going to write about," I said to Gemma as we trailed out of class. "I wish she wouldn't give us such personal homework."

"Well I'm not doing it at all," said Gemma sharply.

"What do you mean?" Gemma *always* did her homework, even when she was off sick. "You have to write something or you'll get a detention."

"I don't care. She can give me a hundred detentions; I'm still not doing it."

"But *why*, Gem? *Why* don't you want to do it?"

"You're not the only one who's lost someone, Maddie," she snapped, her eyes brimming with tears, and she took off down the corridor before I could say anything else.

We had history, second lesson. I tried passing Gemma a note, to ask what was wrong, but Mr Bassington started to hand back our English Civil War projects, walking up and down the aisle, commenting on each one in turn. Gemma had done really well – she got 89%, the highest in the class – but mine didn't even have a mark on it, it just said *Incomplete*.

"You've made a good enough start, Maddie," said Mr Bassington in front of everyone, "but I was expecting so much more."

"Bassington was a bit harsh," said Gemma later. We were in the canteen supposedly having lunch but I was so wound up I couldn't eat a thing. "Are you upset about it?"

I shrugged. "Not really. I knew I hadn't done enough."

"Even so, he didn't have to single you out like that," she said. "Hey, do you want to look at my project? I mean, don't copy it or anything, but you could definitely use it for ideas."

I glanced up at her, surprised. Maybe she felt bad about earlier? She hadn't mentioned it again. She was acting like it never happened.

"Are you sure you wouldn't mind, after all the work you put into it?"

"Of course not! We're friends, aren't we?" She pulled her project out of her bag and handed it to me. "Just don't make it obvious. I really love history, but I know some people find it boring."

"No, I *do* like history, you know I do. It's not that, Gemma, it's just…" She was being so nice, offering me her project…suddenly I wanted to tell her. I should've told her *ages* ago, as soon as Mrs Palmer asked to see me that day. She was my best friend. She'd never judge me or be mean. The only person she was ever mean about was Kieran, and that was only because he was mean to me.

I reached down into my bag, feeling for my ribbon. It helped me just to know it was there, giving me that extra bit of courage I needed. "It's just…I…um…I haven't

158

been coping very well since my nan died. I know it's been months and months and everyone thinks I should be over it by now, but I feel anxious all the time, like something bad's going to happen…"

She leaned forward, nodding, encouraging me to carry on.

"So anyway, I've been finding it really hard to cope. You should've seen my mid-term assessments, my grades were rubbish. That's why I have to go to the Blue Room every Monday and Thursday…"

"What do you mean? For extra lessons?"

"No, not exactly." My face started to heat up. "They're these special sessions run by a counsellor called Vivian. I go there to talk about any worries I might have, stuff like that…"

Gemma took a sip of juice, her eyes never leaving my face. "I wish you'd told me all this before. I feel so stupid. You haven't said anything about your nan, not since you first came back to school, and I've been going on and on about Nathan and rounders club and my new haircut…"

"It doesn't matter. It's not your fault, you didn't know."

She was quiet for a moment and then she grabbed hold of my hand. "Listen, I've got an idea. I know it won't stop you missing your nan or anything, but why don't you come back to mine after school? I'll help you finish your history project and then you can help me to get better at rounders. We'll practise in the garden. My dad's got a cricket bat and I'm sure I've got a tennis ball stashed away somewhere."

I took another big breath, smiling. It was just like Stanley and his new friend at Camp Green Lake, Zero. He teaches Zero how to read and, in return, Zero helps him to dig his hole every day. Vivian was right about scary situations and taking the plunge. I had no idea if it was having my ribbon with me that was helping me, or my sessions with Vivian, but now I'd finally started to open up to Gemma I couldn't believe it had taken me so long.

"Okay," I said, still smiling. "I'll have to ring my mum, but I'm sure she'll say it's fine."

We went back to mine in the end. Mum had to go somewhere straight after work and she needed me home for Charlie. I was relieved in a way. If Gemma was there Mum wouldn't be able to start telling me about this big change, whatever it was. I knew it would have to come out eventually, and a part of me wanted to know, but Mum was right – the way I was feeling at the moment, I wasn't sure I *could* cope with things changing again.

It was the first time Gemma had been round for ages, since before Nan died. I thought it might feel awkward at first but as we walked out of school and down Banner Road, chatting about the history project, and Nathan, and how she was going to get him to notice her at rounders, it felt completely natural, just like it used to. We cut through the cemetery and were almost level with Nan's gravestone when I noticed Kieran. He was sitting on my bench with his knees up and his head down.

I took hold of Gemma's arm and steered her round a different way. I didn't want her to start asking a load of questions about why he was there. I'd not seen him in school all day – he must've bunked off straight after Vivian's session and the row with Sally-Ann. I wondered whether he'd get into trouble; whether anyone cared if he was in school or not.

I hadn't been lying when I said I felt sorry for him. It was almost as if he could disappear down a great big hole and no one would even notice he'd gone.

Rounders practice in the garden was fun. We used an empty plastic bottle for a bat and an old tennis ball and I bowled while Charlie stood behind Gemma as the backstop. Every time she missed, Charlie put his hand over his eyes groaning. I don't think he could believe how bad she was. In the end he ran in to get another bottle and stood next to her to demonstrate.

"You have to keep your eye on the ball," he said, "and start moving your arm back as soon as the ball leaves the bowler's hand. Watch me, okay? Come on, Maddie, bowl the ball."

Charlie's eyes never left the ball as he stood there, his legs so skinny it was difficult to see how they were holding him up. He drew his arm back and whacked the ball with all his strength straight over the fence and into our neighbour's garden.

"That's how you do it," he said, looking quite pleased with himself. "I'll go round and get it back and then you can have another go."

"Oh my god, I *love* Charlie," said Gemma. "I'd totally forgotten how sweet he is. So do you think I'll ever be able to hit it like that?"

"Not unless you wear your glasses! I mean it's difficult to hit something you can't actually see!"

When Charlie came back with the ball, he insisted on training Gemma himself. He bowled over and over until finally after about 500 attempts, she managed to make contact with the ball. It didn't go very far but we all cheered and high-fived each other, then collapsed onto the grass.

It was difficult to read Mum's mood when she got home. She seemed pleased that Gemma was round, really pleased, and it meant neither of us mentioned the row or the fact that I'd rushed off in the morning without breakfast. Charlie kept us entertained all through tea, imitating Gemma's attempts to hit the ball, waving his arms around with his eyes half-closed.

After pudding we went up to my room and Gemma helped me with my project. We got heaps done, almost the whole thing. It was a relief to do something so normal but at the same time I couldn't help listening out for Dad. I was desperate for him to come home, but dreading it at the same time – worried sick about Mum's phone call with Aunty Hat and what was going to happen next.

15
Struggling to Cope

Rounders was a massive disappointment on Wednesday. Nathan was away and it was so unbearably hot that Mr Skinner decided to end the session early.

"All that practice for nothing," moaned Gemma as we trailed out of school. "I've stored everything Charlie taught me in my head, but I'll probably forget it all by next week."

I was going to ask if she wanted to come over again, or suggest going over to hers so we could do our *Holes* homework together, but as we came through the main gates I saw Dad waiting for me, leaning against his van on the other side of the road. I'd barely seen him since his row with Mum the other night. I didn't even know if they'd made up.

"Listen, I've got to go," I muttered. "It's my dad. I'll text you later."

Dad's eyes lit up as I crossed the road. He held his arms out for a hug but I hung back, uncomfortable. He never waits for me after school, not unless I have the dentist or something.

"What do you think of this weather, Maddie?" he said as I climbed in the van. "It's hotter in England today than in Portugal."

I didn't know what to say. He was acting like picking me up was completely normal, as if it was something he did all the time, but there was seriously nothing normal about it. He chatted all the way home about the weather and a job he's been doing and the nightmare he was having with one of his old customers.

"Dad, what's actually going on?" I said as we pulled up outside the house. "Has something happened? Is it Mum or Charlie?"

"No of course not, what do you mean?"

"It's just you never pick me up…you're always at work at this time. Why *aren't* you at work?" I reached into my bag and pulled out my ribbon, my hands trembling slightly.

Dad frowned. "What's that doing in your school bag?"

165

"Nothing, I don't know. Please don't tell Mum..."

"Look, you really don't need it, Mads," he said gently, taking it off me. "There's nothing wrong, I promise. I just wanted to spend some time with you – I've been so busy lately."

Yes, but busy doing what?

"You know, my dad was never around for me much when I was growing up. He was either at work or out at the pub with his mates..."

I stared at him. Dad *never* talked about my granddad. He died before I was born and I hardly know anything about him. Nan didn't talk about him much either. I remember her saying once that he was a quiet man – not a great one for chatting or cuddles.

"The day you were born," Dad went on, "I held you in my arms and I made a promise to myself, and to you, that I wouldn't be like him – distant, difficult to talk to. I didn't want to be that kind of dad."

"You're not," I said. "You're a brilliant dad."

I waited for him to make a joke, lighten the mood, but I'd never seen his face so serious.

"He was in the Scouts when he was a boy, my dad. *Be prepared!* That was his motto. *A good Scout is always prepared.* He was the sort of man who would take an umbrella out on a sunny day, just in case it rained. I'm not kidding, Maddie, it could be as hot as it is today, the middle of summer, not a cloud in sight, but he'd still have his umbrella with him…" He paused for a moment. "But life's not like that, is it?"

"What do you mean?" I said. "I don't understand."

Dad stared down at his hands, fiddling with his keys. "What I mean is, you can't predict when it's going to rain. However prepared you are, you'll always get caught out. You never know when life is going to deliver a surprise…"

My heart began to thump. He was talking about Sharon. He wasn't talking about the weather. He was talking about Sharon getting in touch after so many years. *She* was the surprise. I yanked the ribbon back from him, my heart going a million miles an hour.

"You're talking in riddles," I said. "I don't get what you actually mean…"

"I know, I know, I'm sorry," said Dad, getting flustered. "I'm just trying to say that your granddad didn't like surprises. He liked to know that everything was mapped out and…"

"I don't like surprises either," I said interrupting him. "I hate surprises! *I hate them.* Whatever your surprise is, I don't want to know!"

I yanked the van door open and scrambled out. I didn't want him to tell me. I didn't want to know. I was too frightened. Mum was right. I couldn't cope with one more change.

I let myself in and raced upstairs to my room, slamming the door behind me. Vivian said I'd learn to cope with change over time, but I'd never felt so frightened in my life.

A moment later Charlie burst into my room and flopped down next to me on my bed, hot and sticky in his uniform. He must've heard me come in.

"So how did rounders go? Did Gemma remember what I showed her? Did she manage to hit the ball?"

I shook my head, trying to get my breath back, to calm myself down. "Mr Skinner called it off because of the weather. That's why I'm home early."

"Hey, was that Dad's van I saw just now?" said Mum, popping her head round the door. "What's going on?"

"Nothing, he just came to meet me from school."

"What did he do that for?" She went over to the window, frowning. "Where's he gone now?"

"I'm not sure. I think he just drove off. He's probably gone back to work. I don't even know why he came to pick me up in the first place."

She came over to the bed and squashed herself between the two of us, clocking my ribbon still clenched in my fist. A flicker of worry crossed her face. "Are you okay, Maddie? What did he actually say?"

"I don't know, just something about granddad and the Scouts and how he was always prepared."

"Granddad?" said Mum, almost to herself. "Why on earth was he talking about your granddad?"

I watched her closely. She seemed to be upset, but not *that* upset – not the sort of upset she'd be if Dad was about to leave her. She opened her mouth and then closed it again, as if she wanted to tell me something but decided, for whatever reason, that it would be better if she kept it to herself.

It was almost a relief to get to school the next morning. Dad had spent the whole of breakfast talking football tactics with Charlie. He didn't even mention our conversation in the van – all that stuff about Granddad – but I could feel it hanging in the air between us, waiting to go off like an unexploded grenade.

I had no idea if he'd told Mum about my ribbon either, the fact that he'd seen it in my bag. I was scared she might force me to leave it under my pillow, check before I left the house to make sure I didn't have it with me. There was no way I could face the day without it. So I gulped my cereal down and rushed out before she had the chance to say anything.

Sally-Ann was at the hospital again, so it was just me and Kieran at nurture group. He sat there balancing his stones while I doodled on my pad. Vivian waited to see if either of us was going to start things off and then after about five minutes she said, "Last time you were here, Maddie, you mentioned your nan dying. I was just wondering…had she been ill for a long time?"

I shook my head, swallowing. "No, it was really quick. She had a stroke and she started to recover, but then she got one of those hospital infections and died a week later."

"That must've been a shock, especially as you were close."

"It was horrible," I said, tears springing to my eyes. Nan was still riding around on her bicycle the day before she collapsed. I never even thought of her as old. She was so full of life, always laughing, rushing around from one thing to the next…

Kieran had stopped balancing his stones. He leaned forward, his eyes fixed on my face.

"I didn't even have a week," he said. "My mum was run over, so one minute she was alive and the next minute she was dead." He clicked his fingers. "Just like that."

I breathed in sharply, putting my hand over my mouth. Even though I already knew about his mum, it was still a shock to hear him say it out loud.

"I'm sorry," I whispered. "You must miss her so much."

He stared down at the table, pressing a stone into his hand. One tear rolled down his face, and then another. I looked over at Vivian, waiting for her to do something, but she just let him sit there and cry. After a bit she said, "You've both lost someone you loved and I think that's given you the courage to share those feelings with each other today. It's very frightening to realize that, however hard we try, we can't always control what happens."

I could feel the knots in my stomach loosen for the first time in weeks and weeks, to hear her describe the fear that had been lodged inside me for so long. She offered us both a tissue but Kieran shook his head, wiping his eyes on the back of his sleeve.

"Can I go now?" he said.

It sounded weird. He'd never asked if he could leave before – he usually just got up and walked out whenever he felt like it.

When he'd gone I told Vivian about the day Nan collapsed. How I was with her when it happened, how I tried to call for help but no sound came out, how frightened I'd been to visit her in hospital, how I've always hated hospitals ever since Charlie was born. And I told her about Dad and Sharon and how weird things have been at home. I even told her about bringing my purple ribbon to school and how ashamed it made me feel – how I'd promised myself I'd give it up by the end of term but that since Nan died I needed it more than ever.

I hadn't planned it, I didn't stop to think, I just let it all pour out. It was such a relief – like when you take your bag off after lugging it around all day and realize how much it was weighing you down. She didn't say much, she just let me talk. When I finally ran out of words, she said she appreciated me sharing so much with her – that it must be difficult to get on with normal everyday life when I'd been through such a difficult time and when things were so unsettled at home.

Gemma was waiting for me outside. "How was it?" she said. "Are you okay?"

I nodded, smiling. "I think so. Better than I was yesterday and first thing this morning."

"You're so lucky you've got someone to talk to; someone who can help you…" I was about to ask her what she meant but she rushed on. "Nathan's back, by the way! He walked straight past my locker this morning. I thought he was going to say hi, he sort of opened his mouth like this, but it turned out he was just yawning. Anyway, I cannot *wait* for rounders on Wednesday, even if it is nearly a whole week away. Hey, what are you doing on Saturday?"

I shook my head, struggling to keep up.

"Well I was wondering if you wanted to come into town with me. I could show you where I got my hair cut and then we could go into Boots and try on loads of make-up. Come on, Maddie, please say yes, it'll be so much fun."

I started to say no, but it somehow came out as yes. I didn't want to push her away any more, not when she'd been such a good friend. Maybe if we spent some proper time together, out of school, she'd open up about her own problems. I felt a little flutter of fear in my tummy, like being at home and sitting in the cemetery were my only safe places, but I said yes again, even louder, determined not to back out or let her down.

Kieran was already there when we got to class. He was sitting at the back with his stones out on his desk, his hair flopping down over his face. I looked round at one point and caught him staring at me. Not in the mocking way he used to, it was more intense, as if he was trying to communicate something with his eyes.

"Why does he keep doing that?" said Gemma. "Staring at you in that freaky way? I thought it was just to wind you up, but maybe he fancies you…"

I swivelled back round, my face on fire. "Don't be stupid. Of course he doesn't fancy me, and he's not staring, he just happens to be looking in my general direction."

Gemma laughed. "Are you sure about that, Maddie?"

I laughed along with her, but I wasn't sure about anything to do with Kieran any more.

Gemma and I met at the bus stop at eleven on Saturday. She looked amazing. She'd blow-dried her hair and she was wearing skinny jeans with a short cropped T-shirt and purple high-tops. I could hardly remember what she looked like before. She'd changed so much in the past few weeks – her clothes and haircut and fancying Nathan.

It was really busy in town, especially on the High Street. We tried out loads of make-up in Boots and all their tester perfumes, spraying our wrists so many times we started to get funny looks from the girl behind the counter. Gemma talked me into buying a shimmery blue eyeshadow and she bought a lipgloss for herself, and then we wandered up to a new cafe at the top of the High Street for lunch.

It was brilliant hanging out together. Gemma might look different on the outside but she was still the same old Gemma on the inside. I forgot all about how nervous I'd been. I had my ribbon with me, stuffed at the bottom of my bag, but I didn't feel like getting it out or touching it or anything – it was enough to know it was there, just in case.

"My arm smells rank," said Gemma, sticking her wrist under my nose as we made our way up the road. "It's like a mix between rotten roses and industrial-strength fly killer. Imagine if we bumped into Nathan, right this minute, he'd probably pass out."

"What are you talking about? That's him coming straight towards us, isn't it?"

"Very funny," she said. "I'd know if he was here. I'd be able to sense it."

"What like a Nathan-o-Meter? What happens? Do you start vibrating all over? Or does an alarm go off, like bells ringing or something?"

She pushed me away, laughing. "Just wait until it happens to you, wait until *you* like someone, until *you* hear bells ringing. Then you'll know what I mean!"

The new cafe was so popular people were queuing outside. We stood with our faces pressed against the window.

"Their cakes are supposed to be amazing," said Gemma, practically drooling. "My mum said we should definitely eat here. She's been a few times, but I don't think we'll ever get a table."

"Do you think it's worth waiting?"

"Probably not," she said, turning to go. "Come on, I'm starving."

I was just about to follow her when something stopped me. I'm not even sure what it was, but I pressed my face back against the window, scanning the room.

Gemma pulled my arm. "Come on, Mads, it doesn't matter, we can get a burger or something…"

"Wait a second." I scanned the room one last time and that's when I saw him, sitting with a woman. A woman with a scarf wrapped around her head, a blue silk scarf; her face so close to his it was almost touching. My whole body froze – fingers of ice creeping from my head down to my toes. It was Dad. And he was sitting with the woman from the cemetery.

16
The Girl in the Cafe

"Maddie! What's the matter? Come *on*!" Gemma pulled at my arm again but I couldn't move. There was someone else coming towards the table. A girl, older than me. Long brown hair swept up in a ponytail. I thought I recognized her for a moment, but I wasn't sure. She stopped behind the woman, leaning down to give her a hug.

"*Maddie!* What's wrong? You're scaring me!"

I dragged my eyes away, blinking as if I'd just come out of a deep sleep.

"Sorry, Gemma, it's just that my dad's in the cafe." My voice was shaky. It sounded weird.

"Oh right, do you want to go in and say hi?"

I shook my head.

"You look really pale. Are you sure you're okay?"

"I'm fine. Come on, let's go."

I was scared Dad might look round. I didn't want him to know I'd seen them. What was he doing in a cafe with the woman from the cemetery? The woman I'd been desperate to meet all these weeks. Could she actually be Sharon? And then another thought struck me. Is that why she left the note saying "sorry" on Nan's grave? Because she was taking Dad away from his family? And who was the girl?

I couldn't take it all in. There was so much I didn't understand.

"Do you mind if we go home?" I said.

I didn't want to ruin the day for Gemma, but I was terrified that if we hung around we'd bump into them when they came out. I took off for the bus stop without really waiting for an answer, dragging Gemma along behind me in a frantic effort to get away.

I couldn't relax properly until we were on the bus, and even then it was difficult to get the images out of my head – Dad and that woman in the cafe – the way they were looking at each other, their faces so close. I'd been dying to know who she was for so long, but now I wasn't sure what to think…

"I really wish you'd tell me why you ran off like that," said Gemma, breaking in to my thoughts. "Why didn't you want to say hi to your dad? You're freaking me out, to be honest…"

"I know, I'm sorry, it's just there's something strange going on…" I wiped my palms on my jeans. "Weird stuff that I haven't told you."

She moved closer to me. "What sort of weird stuff?"

I took a breath, forcing myself to speak before I could change my mind. "Well, a couple of weeks ago this woman called Sharon got in touch with my dad. Apparently she used to be his girlfriend, years ago, before he met my mum. They've been seeing each other, meeting up, talking on the phone, and then the other night, when he got home, him and my mum had this massive row…"

"Oh god, Mads, you don't think your mum and dad are going to split up, do you?"

I dug my nails into my hand. It was horrible hearing her say the words out loud, even though I'd been thinking the exact same thing ever since the phone call with Aunty Hat.

"I don't know, but that's not all," I said. "Around the same time as Sharon first called, I was in the cemetery after school one day and I saw a woman standing by my nan's grave. She left a note…"

Gemma squashed even closer to me. "You're kidding. What did it say?"

"It said, *I'm so sorry, forgive me.* She left it with flowers, pink tulips, my nan's favourites. Anyway, the woman was wearing a scarf. It was bright blue silk, wrapped right round her head, like a turban. And then I saw her again, about a week ago, at school. *At Church Vale!* I knew it was her because of the scarf."

"So what happened just now?"

I hesitated. "Um…my dad was with her, in the cafe. The woman from the cemetery with the scarf round her head. He was sitting with her in the cafe, and someone else. A girl. She looked older than us, but not much."

Gemma's eyes were huge behind her glasses. "Are you sure?"

"Positive. And I've got a funny feeling the woman might be Sharon. I think they might be the same person… I can't think of any other explanation…"

"So what are you going to do? Are you going to tell your dad you saw them together?"

I shook my head hard. There was no way I could tell him – it felt shameful, like I'd caught him doing something wrong. I wouldn't even know what to say.

"Look, I'm really sorry the day's been spoiled," I said. "We haven't eaten or anything. You must be starving."

"Don't be silly. We can eat at mine. You will come back with me, won't you? My mum will only start nagging me to do my homework if I go back on my own."

I gave her a shaky smile, trying to squash down the rising panic. "Yeah, I'd love to. I can't face going home on my own either."

It was a relief to be round at Gemma's. It felt calm and normal. Her mum was home and she let us make pizza for lunch, choosing our own toppings. She didn't mention Nan or anything – she just said it was lovely to see me after such a long time. Her dad arrived home while we were eating and stood chatting to us while he ate all of Gemma's pizza crusts.

When we'd finished and cleared away we went up to Gemma's room. She sat me down at her dressing table and made me up using my new eyeshadow and some of her own stuff. She took ages, forcing me to keep my eyes closed so I couldn't see what she was doing. I'd never really worn make-up before, apart from when we did a big show at the end of primary school.

"Okay, you can open them now," she said after what seemed like years. "So come on then, what do you think?"

I sat blinking at my reflection in her dressing-table mirror. It was like staring at a different person. I looked about five years older for a start.

"What's the matter, don't you like it?"

"No I do, I *really* like it; it's just weird – I hardly recognize myself."

"You look beautiful," she said. "Your eyes are amazing."

"No they're not," I said, my face heating up. "Only because you've made them…"

"Hey, look at us here," she interrupted, reaching over my shoulder to grab a strip of photos stuck to her mirror. "I seriously can't believe how much we've changed."

We were in one of those tiny photo booths; our heads squashed together, both of us making silly faces. I remembered the day we took them. It was a Saturday afternoon right at the beginning of Year Seven. We'd gone up to town on our own for the first time, amazed at how grown-up and independent we felt.

"We look *so* young," I said, half-wishing we could go back to that day – actually step inside the picture and be back inside that booth, before Nan's stroke and Dad and Sharon and the woman in the cemetery.

There was something else stuck on Gemma's mirror that I hadn't seen before – one of those scan photos, the kind you get when you're having a baby.

"What's this?" I said.

Gemma didn't answer for a moment. I glanced at her

in the mirror. She was tearing at the skin round her thumb, her cheeks bright red.

"I haven't actually told you…" she said. I turned round to face her. "My mum was pregnant a while back."

"*Pregnant?*"

"Yes, but she, um…she lost the baby. It was a few weeks after your nan died. Mum didn't want me to tell anyone until after she'd had the three-month scan, you know, in case anything went wrong. Anyway she had the scan and it was all fine, but then a couple of days later she started to bleed and she had a miscarriage."

Gemma bowed her head, batting tears away with the back of her hand. "I went with Mum to the scan, Maddie. I saw the baby on the screen. It was horrible when it happened, like losing a real sister or brother."

"Oh god, Gemma, I don't believe it. Why didn't you tell me?"

"I couldn't. Your nan had just died. And then I didn't really know *how* to tell you to be honest. We haven't exactly been close lately."

It was like being punched in the stomach. We'd both been grieving at exactly the same time but I'd been so wrapped up in my own stuff…

"Is that why you were so upset after seeing Mrs Turner's baby? And about the *Holes* homework?"

She nodded. "I nearly told you that day actually, but I think I was worried you wouldn't understand, you know, because it wasn't a *real* baby that had actually died."

"I'm really sorry," I said quietly. "I wish you had told me. It's like with me and Nan. Everyone seemed to be carrying on as normal while I was feeling more and more anxious and I didn't know how to explain, how to put it into words…"

"That's exactly how *I* felt," she said. "No one even knew my mum was pregnant." She shook her head. "I was so upset that day I saw Mrs Turner's baby, I couldn't stop crying. I came home and had a really good talk with my mum. It was the first time I'd actually told her how sad I was feeling."

"It's crazy, Gem. Why didn't we just talk to each other?"

She shrugged, smiling. "I don't know, but I'm really pleased we're talking now."

I smiled back. "Me too. No more secrets, okay?"

"Okay," she said. "Deal."

I felt my phone vibrating in my pocket. It was a text from Mum asking where I was.

"I'd better go," I said. "She was probably expecting me back ages ago."

"So what are you going to do about your dad and the

woman in the cafe?" said Gemma as we went downstairs. "Are you going to confront him, or tell your mum?"

A shudder ran through me at the thought. "I know I should, but I can't. I'm too scared."

She gave me a big hug on the doorstep. "Don't forget. Whatever happens, whatever you decide to do, you can always talk to me."

Dad was at the park with Charlie when I got home; they were having some kind of special training session to make up for all the football they'd missed. I told Mum I wasn't feeling well and edged my way past her and up the stairs. She looked at me for the longest time as if she was trying to decide whether she believed me or not.

"Okay, fine," she said in the end. "I'll come up to see how you are in a bit."

More lies. We were all lying to each other. It was horrible.

I hid away in my room for the rest of the evening. I kept thinking about the woman in the cemetery, how much I'd wanted to talk to her, to find out how she knew Nan and why she was sorry. Now I wanted to know what she was doing in a cafe with my dad on a Saturday afternoon. Was she Sharon? Why else would Dad be meeting her? I couldn't think of any other explanation.

I'd propped up the picture of Nan blowing her candles out on my bedside table, the one I'd brought down from the attic. I picked it up, hugging it to my chest, trying to conjure up her lemony smell, the way her hair frizzed up near her ears, her throaty laugh. If only she was here right now. She'd know what to do. She'd know how to sort everything out.

"*I miss you, Nan,*" I whispered. "*I still miss you so much.*"

17
Charlie's Check-Up

It was Charlie's check-up on Monday. Mum made him a massive breakfast, as if every last calorie mattered, but he pushed his plate away, shaking his head. He hates going to the clinic, especially when they do loads of tests. Dad said he'd take him out for a quick kick-about in the garden if he promised to eat something when he came back in: a bite of toast for every goal.

"You've hardly touched your breakfast either, Mads," said Mum, pouring herself a cup of coffee. "Is your tummy still hurting?"

I nodded and then shook my head. "I don't feel sick or anything, just a bit churned up."

"That's exactly how I feel about Charlie's check-up," she said, as if my churned-up tummy didn't really count, as if *I* didn't count. She shook her head, sighing. "It's always the same, every time, even though we've been going to the clinic for years. I know I won't properly relax until it's over."

Sometimes I wonder what it would've been like if Charlie hadn't been premature, if he'd been born three months later, like a normal baby, if things might be different between me and Mum. I had an overwhelming urge suddenly to shout in her face or shake her really hard, to remind her that she had two children and they *both* needed her.

"Did you know Gemma's mum was pregnant?" I said. I don't know why – I just blurted it out. "Gemma told me yesterday when I was at her house. Her mum had a miscarriage just after her first scan."

"No, I had no idea," said Mum, shaking her head. "Christina never said. The poor thing. Was Gemma very upset?"

"Very. It happened around the same time as Nan died."

Mum picked up her coffee and blew on it. "I thought I was having a miscarriage with Charlie," she said quietly. I tensed up. Charlie *again*, it was so frustrating. "I knew it was too early," she went on, "much too early. I just

188

remember being terrified I was going to lose him…"

She trailed off, staring past my shoulder as if she was remembering the day it happened. "I felt so guilty, Mads. As if it was my fault the pregnancy had gone so wrong… as if I'd done something to cause it…eaten the wrong thing, worked too hard…"

"I told Vivian about it," I said. "At nurture group."

Mum's eyes flickered back to my face. "What do you mean? What did you tell her?"

"Just about Charlie being born too early, how much you worry about him…"

"Oh…" Mum looked surprised, as if it had never occurred to her that her worries might affect me so much. "And what did she say?"

I opened my mouth to answer, to tell Mum how Vivian said it must've been a very anxious time for me as well, that I must've wondered what happened to the mum I'd had *before* Charlie was born – but just then Charlie came stumbling back in from the garden.

"Dad says my shots have got much stronger!" he said, as Dad came in behind him. "I don't see why I have to even *go* to the clinic now. You could just ring them up and tell them how much better I am…"

Mum sighed, looking past him at Dad. "Of course you have to go," she said. "It's not just about your legs,

Charlie, you know that. Come on, sit down and have something to eat." She jumped up to put some more bread in the toaster, totally focused on Charlie again. "I'm pleased about your shots, though," she added, turning back to give him a quick hug. "Wait until Mr Maddox sees…he might even choose you for the team!"

Kieran was standing outside the Blue Room as I came up the corridor to nurture group, his hand hovering over the doorknob. I hung back for a moment, embarrassed. It was the first time I'd seen him since he told me and Vivian about his mum, but he looked just as angry as usual, his shoulders hunched up around his ears.

He swung round suddenly, as if he'd decided to leave, but then he saw me and froze. I wasn't sure what to do. For some weird reason I really wanted him to stay.

"Come on then," I muttered, sort of nodding at the door. He shook his head, still frozen to the spot. "Come on, Kieran," I tried again. "Vivian will be waiting for us."

"I can't," he muttered. "I can't do it any more."

"Yes you can," I said a bit more firmly. "You have to."

I reached past him and opened the door, hoping he'd follow me in. I don't even know why it mattered so much to me, but it did.

Sally-Ann was already in there talking away to Vivian. I grabbed my pad and sat across from her in my usual seat. Kieran waited for another moment or two and then shuffled in, sitting as near to the door as he could get, as if he wasn't planning to stay for very long.

"We've got a French test this morning," Sally-Ann was saying. "But I don't actually think I should have to take it because I was away last week, and anyway I'm rubbish at French."

I doodled RUBBISH at the top of the page and began to list all the things I was rubbish at: *coping with change, confronting Dad, talking to Mum, coming to school without my ribbon…*

"Perhaps you're worried that if you take the French test, you'll be just like everyone else, and the French teacher will forget how poorly you've been," said Vivian.

Sally-Ann frowned. "What do you mean? Do you think I'm using my illness to get out of it?"

I glanced up at Kieran. He was staring at me again, that same intense look. I wanted to take my ribbon out of my bag but I was too embarrassed.

"No, I don't think that," said Vivian. "It's just that all three of you are dealing with some serious issues that set you apart – and while I'm sure you wish you could be the same as everyone else, sometimes there can be a comfort in holding on to what makes us different."

"I still don't understand," said Sally-Ann.

"Nor do I," I said, wondering what possible comfort there was in being anxious all the time. Needing my purple ribbon just to get through the day.

Vivian thought for a moment. "Well, let's say your tummy was all better, Sally-Ann, no more nasty pains or hospital appointments, you might be scared that we wouldn't worry about you any more." She turned to face me. "And, Maddie, you might be scared that if we thought you were *over* your nan – if you began to relax, even for a moment, went back to being the happy, chatty Maddie you used to be – you might get another shock. Things might change again and you wouldn't be able to cope."

But things are already changing, I thought. *And everyone knows I can't cope.*

"What about me then?" said Kieran, sneering. "What am I scared of?"

"I think you're frightened," said Vivian, in the gentlest voice I'd heard her use, "that if you allowed yourself to trust us, to let us in, even a tiny bit, you might get hurt all over again."

Kieran scraped back his chair, standing up. "The only thing I'm frightened of," he said, "is staying here listening to this crap."

He took a step towards the door, his hands thrust deep into his pockets.

"It's easy to walk away when things get tough," said Vivian, "when I say things you don't like. It's so much harder to stay."

Kieran took another step towards the door and then hesitated. I held my breath. *Stay,* I thought. *Please stay*.

"Walking out is always an option, Kieran," Vivian went on. "No one is forcing you to stay. But if you keep on doing that, if you keep on shutting us out, nothing will change."

He thrust his hands even deeper into his pockets, his shoulders hunched up to his ears. And then slowly, as if he couldn't quite believe he was doing it, he turned round and slunk back to his chair. He stayed for the rest of the session – he didn't say anything but it felt massive, like he was admitting for the first time that he needed Vivian's help.

I didn't say much either; Sally-Ann did most of the talking. She was telling Vivian about her mum's new boyfriend. She said she hated it when her mum started seeing someone new, that it was so obvious they didn't want her around.

"I expect you've been used to having your mum all to yourself," said Vivian.

"Only when she's single," said Sally-Ann. "As soon as

she meets someone new, it's bye-bye, Sally-Ann…" She broke off, holding her side as if she was in pain. "I've got such a bad tummy-ache," she said. "I'm not making it up, I swear. It's right here…"

"I wonder if what you're *really* saying is that it hurts to share your mum with her new boyfriend?"

Sally-Ann squeezed her eyes tight. "Yes it does," she whispered. "It really hurts."

"I have that exact feeling," I said suddenly. "It's because I don't want to share my dad."

I put my hands up to my cheeks; they were red-hot. I had no idea I was going to say that, it just came out. I couldn't help it. The thought of sharing Dad with someone other than Mum and Charlie was unbearable.

Sally-Ann opened her eyes. I thought she was going to say that her pain was worse than mine or something, but she didn't, she just gave me a tiny smile. I glanced over at Kieran but he was busy balancing his stones, concentrating hard as he placed one on top of the other. As soon as he'd placed the last one, taking ages to make sure it was in exactly the right position, he flicked the tower with his finger, scattering the stones across the table.

When he got up to leave at the end of the session, Vivian said, "Thank you for staying, Kieran, it was extremely brave."

"Whatever!" he said without even looking at her. But he didn't sound angry.

Vivian was right; it was brave of him to stay, the bravest thing ever, trusting Vivian enough to sit back down. I couldn't help feeling like I was the coward. I was the one who was too scared to face up to what was happening at home, to cope with everything changing again. I suddenly got this image of my granddad taking his umbrella out with him every day, just in case it rained.

Gemma was waiting for me right outside. "You didn't miss much at registration," she said. "Mrs Palmer went on about the boys' toilets for a change, and said she needs volunteers for the summer fair. We could run a stall together if you like…"

I was only half-listening. I was still thinking about Vivian and what she said, wondering if I could be as brave as Kieran – if I could find the courage to go home after school and tell Dad I'd seen him in the cafe, however difficult it was. I didn't want to be *Maddie Mouse* any more. I didn't want to be like my granddad.

"How was the session?" said Gemma as we walked towards our lockers. "Did you tell Vivian what's been going on?"

I shook my head. "It's not really like that, but she did say something about me being scared and…" I stopped mid-sentence. The bird in my chest began to flap about like crazy. There was a girl standing by my locker. Long brown hair swept up in a ponytail. It was her. The girl I'd seen on Saturday. The girl from the cafe.

18
Running Away

"Hey!" I shouted, without thinking. Her head snapped up and she took off down the corridor. "Wait! Don't go!"

I ran after her, pushing past people, desperate to keep her in my view, but she was too fast. She turned the corner at the end of the corridor and disappeared, swallowed up by a whole crowd of Year Tens coming out of registration.

I stood there, breathing hard. It was definitely her, I was sure of it. Why was she standing by my locker? Why did she take off like that? And what had she been doing in the cafe with my dad? The questions ricocheted around my head until it was impossible to think straight. I heard

Gemma call out behind me but I felt dizzy and sick and I had to be alone.

I hurried down the corridor, straight past the Blue Room and round the corner, and then slipped into the nearest loo, locking myself in one of the cubicles, trying to take a proper breath, to calm myself down. I fumbled around in my bag for my ribbon. I needed to hold it, to breathe it in. My fingers were trembling as I searched every corner, unzipping all the pockets. Where was it? *Where was it?*

I began to feel light-headed, as if my brain needed more oxygen, as if I couldn't take a deep-enough breath. I pulled everything out of my bag, desperate to find it. I was absolutely certain I'd put it in there this morning. It had to be here. How was I supposed to cope without it?

The door banged open suddenly making me gasp out loud.

"The bell's rung! Come on, you'll be late for class!"

It was one of the hall monitors. I sat rigid, praying for them to leave. I didn't know what to do. I couldn't go to class. I couldn't carry on the day as if nothing had happened. I needed to talk to Vivian, to tell her about the girl and how panicky I was feeling, how I'd left my ribbon at home. She'd understand. She'd know what to do.

As soon as I heard the door swing shut I stuffed

everything back in my bag, stumbled out of the loo and ran back towards the Blue Room. I stood outside for about five minutes working out what I should say. I had no idea if Vivian was still in school, or if she'd even agree to see me. I wiped my hands on my skirt, took a deep, shaky breath and knocked. There was the sound of a chair scraping back and then a moment later the door opened.

"Oh, hello, Maddie. Did you forget something?"

I shook my head, my heart beginning to race again. There was someone else in the room – a younger boy from Year Seven. My tummy clenched up. It never occurred to me that Vivian might see other pupils while she was here. For some reason I thought she only came to Church Vale to see me and Sally-Ann and Kieran.

"Is everything okay, Maddie? If you need to talk some more I'll be free at lunchtime…"

I shrank back, shaking my head again. "It's nothing," I muttered. "I'm fine."

Vivian had made me feel special. She'd made me feel as if my problems mattered like Nan used to, but now it was only fifteen minutes after my session and she was already listening to someone else. She was just doing her job. She didn't really care. Not about me or Sally-Ann or Kieran.

I turned and ran down the corridor. I had to get out.

It felt as if everything was closing in on me. There was no one to talk to, no one who really cared. I ran straight past the hall monitors and out of the side exit before they could say anything. I had no idea if they would follow me or alert someone. I'd never done anything like this before in my life.

I didn't stop running until I was out of the school grounds and right at the bottom of Banner Road. When I looked back the way I'd come, the road seemed to stretch on for miles. I felt very far away suddenly, as if I was lost, even though I knew exactly where I was. I crouched down in the street, scared and shaky, wishing I'd stayed at school. I should've waited until the end of English, told Gemma about seeing the girl. Now I'd be in trouble for skipping school, and Mum would find out and everything would be a million times worse.

As soon as my legs felt strong enough to carry me, I trailed into the cemetery and down the path towards Nan's grave. There were a few other people around but not many. I sat on the bench, pulling my knees up to my chest, trying to make sense of everything – wishing I had my ribbon with me, trying to remember the last time I felt truly safe.

I must've been sitting there for about five minutes when I sensed someone coming up the path towards me.

It took a moment to realize it was Kieran. He looked furious – I could almost feel the anger coming off him. I shrank back, hugging my knees even tighter.

"What the hell are you doing here?" he snarled as he reached the bench. "You'd better not be following me!"

"F…f…following you?" I stammered. "Why would I be following you? I told you. M…m…my nan's buried in this cemetery."

"Aren't you supposed to be in English right about now?"

"Aren't *you?*"

I thought he was going to hit me for a minute. His fists were clenched by his side, his shoulders hunched up. I shrank even further into the bench until I could feel the wooden slats digging into my skin through my shirt. Why hadn't I kept my mouth shut? Just because he'd opened up a bit at nurture group didn't mean he'd suddenly morphed into a different person.

He stood there, eyes fixed on mine, as if he was working out what he was going to do to me. And then the weirdest thing happened. He smiled. I blinked a few times, convinced I was seeing things. Kieran Black was standing in front of me *smiling*.

"What?" I said, sick of him, sick of being scared, sick of *everything*. "What's the big joke?"

"Nothing."

"Do you think I'm funny or something?" Anger was bubbling up inside me, burning my throat.

"Calm down, I wasn't laughing at you. I just didn't think you were the type to skip school, that's all."

I shrugged. "Me neither…"

"You should go back," he said. "You'll get into trouble."

"What about you? How come you never get into trouble for skipping?"

"No one cares what I do." His voice was flat as if he didn't care much either. I stared up at him, trying to read his face, trying to work out what I could say, but he grabbed hold of my arm suddenly, pulling me up from the bench.

"Follow me!" he hissed. "Don't say anything and don't look back." He dragged me up the path and then started to walk very fast, breaking into a run.

"What's the matter? Where are we going?" I stumbled along behind him, struggling to keep up.

"Faster!" he hissed. "Hurry up!" He didn't slow down until we were out of the cemetery and halfway up Amberly Road. "Come on. I know a place where we can hide."

"What are you talking about?" I pulled back. "You're scaring me, Kieran. Hide from what?"

He swung round to face me, his eyes flashing fear.

"It was my dad – he was walking straight towards us and he's been drinking. Now come *on*, let's go!"

He led me down an alley between some houses. It was overgrown with blackberry bushes and nettles and I had to hold my arms up high to avoid being stung. The first alley led into another and then another, until I'd lost all sense of where I was. Kieran obviously knew exactly where he was going. He strode along in front of me until we reached an old wooden gate leading into some woods.

"I have no idea where we are," I said, leaning against the gate, hot and clammy, my shirt sticking to my back. "I didn't even know there were woods here."

"It's just another entrance to Hadley Heath. If we walk all the way through the woods and out the other side we won't be far from school." He climbed onto the gate and jumped over. "Come on…we'd better go. It doesn't take long."

I climbed over after him and we trailed through the woods side by side. It felt weird. Not like we were friends but not like we were enemies either. I was dying to ask him about his dad and why he'd reacted like that when he saw him, but I was scared he might get angry and storm off – leave me here in the middle of nowhere all by myself.

"I've never done anything like this before," I said in

the end, to break the silence. "It's just that something happened at school and I sort of freaked out…"

"No, it's not like Maddie Mouse to do something so naughty!"

"I am *not* a mouse," I said. But he was smiling again, teasing me. My tummy flipped over. I couldn't get used to this new, smiling Kieran. It was like entering a parallel universe. I felt a bit light-headed, but not like before, not in a scary way – more like if Kieran Black could joke around with me, then anything could happen.

"Sometimes I spend all day here," said Kieran, breaking into my thoughts, "if my dad's at home, or at the cemetery. I come here to get away from him."

"Is he drunk all the time?"

He leaned down to pick up a stick, dragging it along the ground as we walked on. "Not all the time. He can be fine for ages and then something sets him off and he flips."

"Are you scared of him?"

He shrugged. "Not really. I know how to handle him when he's been drinking."

I wondered if that was true. The fear in his eyes when he pulled me out of the cemetery seemed real enough. We followed the path until the woods thinned out and we were on the heath. It was a relief to recognize where we were, although I wasn't in any big hurry to go back to school.

We made our way across the grass; it was dry and yellow, desperate for rain. I couldn't believe I was on Hadley Heath with Kieran Black and it felt so normal. A few weeks ago I was frightened to be in the same room as him. The field sloped upwards, higher and higher. I followed behind him, struggling to keep up and drenched in sweat, but it was worth it when we got to the top. The view was incredible.

Kieran flopped down on the grass, and then lay back staring up at the sky. It was so hot you could almost see the heat shimmering above us.

"I used to come up here with my mum," he said. His voice was quiet and I had to strain to hear him properly. "This was her favourite spot. She used to say it was like being right on top of the world."

I sat down next to him, shocked that he'd said something so personal.

"Do you believe in heaven, Maddie?" he went on. "Do you think there's some perfect place where all the dead people go?"

I pulled at the grass, worried I might say the wrong thing. It felt massive that he would even talk about his mum; the last thing I wanted to do was to make him feel worse.

"Um, I'm not sure to be honest. Sometimes I think my nan's in heaven and it's a really happy feeling, like eating doughnuts on a summer's day." I rushed on, embarrassed, "But at other times it's just this horrible black space and everything feels empty and hopeless."

I didn't mention the times I'd actually seen her, or *thought* I'd seen her, on the rounders field and in the kitchen. I didn't want him to think I was completely unhinged.

"I don't believe in heaven, or in God," he said more harshly. "I only go to the cemetery to keep her grave tidy, but I feel much more connected to my mum when I'm up here."

I wished there was something I could do to make him feel better, some way to stop him feeling so alone. He didn't say anything else after that; he just lay there. It was so peaceful, like someone had turned the sound off. I would've been happy to stay there all day, but eventually he got up and we started to make our way down the hill and towards the exit.

"I'm not going back to school," he said when we got to the gate. "I'll probably hang around here for a while and then head home."

"Won't you get into trouble?"

"Not really. I told you before, no one cares."

He turned back the way we'd come, trailing the stick behind him. I wanted to tell him that people did care. That I cared. That he didn't have to face everything alone.

"Hey, Kieran…"

He turned round. His eyes were cold again, his shoulders hunched up to his ears. The words sounded stupid suddenly – I couldn't bring myself to say them.

"Nothing," I muttered. "I'll see you tomorrow."

19
Facing Mum

Sneaking back into school was much harder than running out. I had to sign in for a start. I was just filling in my name and the time when Mrs Palmer came hurrying down the corridor towards me.

"There you are, Maddie! Where on earth have you been? You can't just leave school without letting us know! Did you have an appointment or something?"

I nodded, hoping that would be enough to get rid of her, but she wanted loads more information: what time I'd left, why Mum hadn't rung up to inform the school, and what my appointment was for. I think she knew I was lying but eventually she let me go to my next class. It was

RE and Gemma had saved me a seat. Her face lit up when she saw me, as if I'd been missing for days.

"Where've you been?" she whispered. "You just ran off down the corridor and disappeared! What happened? Was it to do with your counselling session?"

I shook my head. "It was the girl from the cafe…"

"What do you mean? Here at Church Vale?"

"Yes, I saw her standing by my locker…" Miss Beckford the RE teacher shot us a look. "Listen, I'll tell you later, okay?"

I had no idea what the lesson was about or what I was supposed to be doing. I stared out of the window, wondering where Kieran was. I wanted to be back on the heath with him, gazing up at the sky, as far away from my real life as I could possibly get.

The day dragged on but it must've felt even longer for Kieran, waiting for school to be over before he went home to his dad. Someone should be doing something to help him. It was so unfair that he had to cope with losing his mum *and* with his dad being drunk all the time. I wondered if anyone at school knew what he was really going through.

Mrs Palmer caught up with me just before the end of the day and asked me to stay behind for a moment. She said it wouldn't take long, but I could tell from her face that it was serious. Gemma wanted to wait for me but I said I'd text her later.

"I had to call your mum, I'm afraid, Maddie," Mrs Palmer said as soon as everyone else had left. "She didn't know anything about an appointment and obviously she was very concerned that you'd left the building in the middle of the day…" She trailed off, her head on one side, expecting me to say something, to explain.

"I'm sorry," I said, staring down at my hands. Mum would go mad. The last thing she needed was something else to worry about, especially today when Charlie had his appointment. "I didn't mean to lie."

Mrs Palmer reached out and rubbed my arm. "Look, I understand that things are difficult for you right now, but seriously, Maddie, if you're upset or worried about anything, anything at all, you've got to come and talk to me, let me know how you're feeling. You can't just run out of school."

"I know, and I will. I just didn't know what else to do."

Mrs Palmer opened the green file on her desk, the one with my name on the front, running her eyes over the first page.

"You've been part of Vivian's nurture group for a few weeks now," she said. "Do you think it's helping? I did talk to her this afternoon and she said she felt you were gaining a lot from the sessions. I can see for myself that you've been finding it easier to talk…"

I nodded, desperate to get away. I needed to explain to Mum, to try and make her understand.

"Can I go now?" I whispered.

"Yes, of course. Come on, I'll walk down with you."

Mum was standing by the office, arms folded across her chest, her face closed up, impossible to read. Mrs Palmer hung back as I rushed towards her.

"I'm sorry," I said. "I didn't mean to worry you."

"Running out of school, Maddie! Honestly! I couldn't believe it when Mrs Palmer rung me. Charlie was right in the middle of his check-up at the clinic – did you even think of that? Today of all days! Where on earth did you go?"

I shrank back. I hated it when she used that voice, looked at me like that. I wanted her to hug me, not tell me off. "J…just down to the cemetery," I stammered, blinking back tears. "I'm really sorry, I won't do it again."

"I'd better have a quick word with Mrs Palmer," she said, her voice a bit softer. "Please don't shut me out, Maddie. We can get through this, we *will* get through it, but you need to talk to me. Running away isn't going to solve anything."

I promised Mum and Mrs Palmer that I'd never leave

school again. That if I was worried about anything I'd make sure I told someone. Mrs Palmer said she wanted me to understand that no one was angry and that my safety was all that mattered. Finally we were in the car and driving away. I pressed my face against the window as we drove past the cemetery but there was no sign of Kieran, or his dad.

As soon as we got in I rushed upstairs to find my ribbon. It was still tucked under my pillow from last night. I must've forgotten to put it in my bag before we left for school. I sank down onto my bed, holding it up to my face, breathing it in, going over everything that had happened since I saw the girl standing by my locker: running out of school, Kieran's dad in the cemetery, climbing up to the top of the heath...

"Come on, Maddie." Mum popped her head round the door. "I've got the kettle on. We need to talk."

I trailed downstairs, working out what I could say, how I could make Mum understand. She gave me a small smile as I came into the kitchen. It was difficult to know if she was still cross, or just worried.

"I dropped Charlie round at Rory's after the clinic," she said, nodding for me to sit down next to her at the table. "I wasn't sure how long we'd be up at school and, anyway, I wanted the chance to talk to you alone." She paused to take a sip of her tea. "Look, I know I've said this before, Maddie, but I'm worried about how much time you're spending at the cemetery..."

"It's not really about the cemetery," I said, frustrated. "I just get this feeling sometimes, a sort of frightened, out-of-control feeling like I can't cope. Something happened at school and I got upset and then I got in a panic because I couldn't find my ribbon..." The words were out before I could stop them.

"*Your ribbon?*" Mum frowned. "What do you *mean*? Since when have you been taking your ribbon to school?"

I shrivelled under her gaze. Why did I always feel like I was letting her down? "I don't. I didn't, not until...um... not until the other week."

"But *why*, Maddie? What happened? I thought you were getting better. I thought the sessions with Vivian were helping: joining the rounders club, Gemma coming over..." She trailed off, pinching the bridge of her nose.

She didn't get it. She just didn't understand. *What about the phone call to Aunty Hat?* I felt like screaming. *What about Dad and Sharon?* The sessions with Vivian *had* started to help. I *had* begun to open up and talk about my feelings – but how on earth did Mum expect me to get better with all this other stuff going on at home?

"At least I can *talk* to Vivian!" I said, pushing my chair

back from the table and standing up. "At least she actually listens to me, just like *Nan* used to listen to me. You're so worried about Charlie all the time – Charlie's check-up and Charlie growing and Charlie getting on the football team…" Tears welled up but I batted them away. "I mean, I get it. I get that he needs extra care and stuff, but what about me? What about what *I* need? You don't even know I exist half the time!"

Mum looked as if I'd slapped her. She opened her mouth and closed it again. "Maddie, I'm…I don't… I didn't realize…"

"Just forget it," I said, too angry and upset to listen to her excuses. "I don't want to talk about it any more."

Mum stood up too and reached out to me, pulling me into her arms for a hug. "You're right, Maddie," she said. "Seriously, I feel terrible. I've really let you down. I'm so used to worrying about Charlie; sometimes I forget just how much you need me too."

I thought I was hearing things for a moment. It was the first time she'd ever said anything like that. The words wrapped themselves round me like a warm blanket.

"I'll make it up to you, Mads," she went on. "I know things haven't been easy for you since your nan died but I'll make it up to you, I promise."

We stayed at the table for a while after that, just

drinking tea and chatting about school and rounders club and how I was getting on with Vivian. I knew I should ask her about the woman in the cafe, force her to tell me the truth, but it was so nice to spend some proper time together, with Mum focused on me for a change rather than Charlie, I couldn't bring myself to spoil the moment.

Rory's mum dropped Charlie home a bit later. He told me all his news over dinner. He'd managed to grow two centimetres since his last check-up and, even more exciting than that, Mr Maddox had decided to hold new football trials for the last few games of the season. When Dad arrived home from work Charlie leaped up to meet him at the front door, dragging him straight into the garden to practise.

"This is my big chance!" he said as they disappeared outside. "I'm determined to get picked this time, to show Mr Maddox what I can do! To prove to him that I'm as good as the others…"

Mum glanced across the table at me, rolling her eyes. "If only all our problems were as easy to solve, eh, Maddie?"

* * *

I was dreading school the next morning, petrified I might see the girl again. A part of me was desperate to know who she was, but every time I imagined coming face-to-face with her my legs turned to jelly. It was a nightmare getting to class. I waited for the corridors to clear just to be sure I wouldn't bump into her.

I got to English a few minutes late. Miss Owen gave me a look but she didn't say anything. Kieran was sitting at the back with his stones out, his hair hanging down over his eyes. It was strange to see him after yesterday. I had no idea how things would be between us, if he'd pretend it never happened. It didn't even feel real any more – more like something I'd dreamed up.

The rest of the class had their copies of *Holes* open on their desks. We were up to the part where Stanley and Zero run away from Camp Green Lake. The conditions are gruelling and at one point Stanley has to carry Zero up the side of the mountain when he becomes too weak to walk. We read the chapter out loud and then Miss Owen asked us to think about what lengths we would go to for a friend.

"I know it's not the same as Stanley and Zero," whispered Gemma, "but I swear I'll help you find out what's going on with your dad, why he was in the cafe with that girl…"

I gave her a shaky smile to show how much it meant to me.

"Do you think you'd recognize her if you saw her again?"

I nodded. "Definitely. But there are over 1,500 pupils at Church Vale and we don't even know which year she's in…"

"Girls, I hope you're talking about the book," said Miss Owen. "What lengths would you go to for a friend, Maddie? You've obviously got lots to say on the subject…"

I couldn't believe she was asking me; I had no idea what to say. The bird began to flap its wings again. It was like an automatic response. I opened my mouth but the words were stuck in my throat, blocking it up, making it difficult to breathe. Everyone was staring at me, waiting. I thought I'd been getting better but it was just as bad as before. I glanced at the door, desperate to run out.

"Well I'll tell you what lengths *I'd* go to for a friend," said Kieran suddenly, in his loudest, most obnoxious voice. Miss Owen swung round, frowning. "I'd go about thirty-three centimetres, or if I was feeling particularly energetic I might go thirty-four or even thirty-five. Would that be far enough?"

The entire class cracked up laughing.

"Thank you, Mr Black, that was extremely *un*helpful,"

said Miss Owen, her voice like ice. "Stay behind after class to talk to me and if anyone else wants to join him they'd be most welcome. Now read up to page 181 in silence."

There were a few more snorts and sniggers and then, slowly, heads went down. Kieran had saved me. He'd called out on purpose to distract Miss Owen.

"What an idiot," hissed Gemma.

But as soon as it was safe I twisted round to the back and mouthed thank you, my cheeks flaming. His eyes met mine, a hint of a smile crossing his face. I couldn't believe he'd done that for me. He'd probably get a detention or worse.

I had no idea what happened with Miss Owen at the end of the lesson but he didn't show up for any of his classes that afternoon. I could guess where he was – sitting up at the top of the heath thinking about his mum. I was tempted to disappear too – run out of school and never come back. But deep down inside I knew I couldn't run away for ever.

20
Kieran in Trouble

I didn't see Kieran again until the next day, after school at rounders club. It's not that he was there exactly; I just spotted him walking past while our team was waiting to bat. He stopped at the end of the field, right by the sycamore trees, his hands thrust deep into his pockets.

"Your boyfriend's come to watch," teased Gemma. "I hope you're going to score a rounder for him."

"He's not my boyfriend," I said, turning crimson. "I don't know why you keep saying that!"

"Well what's he doing here then? I mean he hasn't been to any classes today and then he turns up to watch rounders. Seriously, he's so weird."

"He's not weird! You just don't know him. And anyway, what about *your* boyfriend?"

Nathan was back and Gemma was determined to show him how good she was. She'd been going on about it all day, trying to remember Charlie's tips. I was desperate for her to hit the ball, even if it didn't go very far. She was convinced it was the only way she was going to get him to notice her.

"Don't forget to start moving your arm back before the ball leaves the bowler's hand," I said, as she got up to bat. "And make sure you keep your eye on the ball as it's coming towards you…"

"That's if I can see it," she said, leaning back down and slipping her glasses into my hand.

"*Gemma!*"

"*Shhhh!*" She put her finger up to her lips. "Don't put me off, Maddie! I'm trying to concentrate."

The ball flew straight past her before she could even focus, let alone move her arm. The backstop flung it towards first base and she was out.

"What do you mean, out?" she said, looking over at Nathan. "That's not fair, I wasn't ready!"

"You have to run, Gemma," he said, rolling his eyes. "You can't just stand there even if you miss."

It was my turn next. I glanced across the field as I

got up. Kieran was still there, standing right in front of the sycamore trees at the far end of the field. The exact same place I'd seen Nan. I had no idea if she'd be there again, but I couldn't help worrying that he was in her way, blocking her view – that I wouldn't be able to hit the ball if she couldn't see me.

"Come on, Maddie," said Nathan. "We desperately need a rounder here."

I tried to pretend Kieran wasn't there, focusing on the ball as it came speeding towards me. So what if he was watching, it's not as if it was against the law or anything. And who said he was there because of me anyway? He was probably just hanging around at school to avoid going home to his dad.

There was a deafening crack as the ball made contact with the bat.

"*Run*, Maddie, *run!*" yelled Nathan – and the rest of the team began to chant, "Mad-die! Mad-die!"

I raced from first, to second and then straight to third. I was moments away from scoring my first rounder. My lungs were bursting – I'd never run so fast in my life. One of the fielders flung the ball towards Chloe on fourth base, but it was too late. She fumbled the catch and I slid into the base before she could do anything about it.

There was a huge cheer as I made my way back to my

team, out of breath and grinning. Gemma was going mad – jumping up and down, her arms pumping the air. "You did it, Maddie! You actually got a rounder! I'm so, so jealous!"

I glanced across the field to see if Kieran was still there, to see if he'd watched me score, but it was as if he'd disappeared into thin air.

Our team went on to win by one rounder. The final score was 7–6. Mr Skinner actually came over to congratulate me. He said I had fantastic hand-eye coordination or something, and that he hoped I'd sign up for the school rounders team next year.

"You basically won the match for us," said Gemma. "I just don't get how you can hit it so far – you're like one of the smallest on the team…"

I was still grinning as we walked out of school. I might be one of the smallest but right at that moment I felt as if I could achieve anything. I'd never dreamed I'd be good enough for the school team, let alone be *asked* to join, and I'd done it all by myself, without any help from Nan.

I was about to ask Gemma if she wanted to come over for another practice in the garden when I noticed Dad's van parked just outside the main gates. My tummy flipped over. I'd managed to avoid him at home over the past couple of days – pretty much since spotting him in the cafe – torn between wanting to know what was going on and being scared of the truth. But there was no escaping him now.

"Let's go," I said without thinking. "It's my dad again but I really don't want to talk to him." I grabbed Gemma's arm and we walked straight past. I heard the door open but I didn't stop.

"Maddie!" he called. "Hang on!"

"What are you going to do?" hissed Gemma, rushing to keep up. "Do you want to go back?"

My eyes welled up but I was determined not to cry. "No, it's okay. Just keep walking."

"But maybe you *should* talk to him?"

The van restarted and Dad cruised past us, pulling in just ahead. He got out and stood on the pavement, his arms folded across his chest. I thought about crossing the road but I couldn't bear to see the hurt on his face.

"I think I should go," said Gemma. "Text me later."

She gave me a quick hug and hurried on past Dad's van and down the road.

"What's the matter?" said Dad as soon as she was out of earshot. "Why didn't you stop?"

I stood rooted to the spot.

"Come on, Maddie, please. We need to talk."

I didn't know what to do. I couldn't move. I couldn't face hearing the truth.

"Please, Maddie; I've left work specially…"

I opened my mouth, struggling to find the right words, to explain how frightened and confused I was, to make him understand how much I needed him, how scared I was that he didn't want to be part of our family any more, that everything was changing again.

"Do you still love me?" was all I managed in the end.

It sounded so pathetic, like I was three years old or something.

Dad's face sagged. "Of course I still love you. How can you even ask?"

He held out his arms and walked towards me, wrapping me up in the tightest hug. We stood like that for what seemed an age. I could feel the tension seeping out of my body. It felt so warm and safe. I wished I could stay there for ever.

"There's something I need to tell you, Maddie," he said into my hair. "Something really important…"

"Okay," I said, closing my eyes, steeling myself for the truth, determined not to wimp out this time. But before he could say anything else his phone started to ring.

"I'm sorry, love, it must be work," he said, stepping back from me slightly. "Hang on a sec, I'll switch it off."

He pulled his phone out of his pocket, frowning at the screen. I stepped back a bit further, watching his face carefully. "I'm sorry," he said again, "but I've got to get this." He turned away, cupping his hand over his mouth so I couldn't hear, but I didn't hang around to listen anyway. It was Sharon. It had to be.

I took off down the road as fast as I could. Why did he have to answer? Why couldn't he let it ring? What was the point of being brave and facing up to things if he was going to put Sharon first? I heard him call out and then the van starting up, but I cut through the cemetery so he couldn't follow. I didn't stop running until I reached my bench, collapsing down out of breath, fighting back tears.

There was a funeral at the far end of the cemetery and the mourners were huddled together, clutching tissues and holding onto each other for support. I felt like crying along with them. I sat and watched as the vicar said a short prayer before the coffin was lowered into the ground.

As the crowd began to clear, I noticed Kieran. He was standing behind them, watching the funeral from the other side. I raised my hand to wave at him and he trailed over, dodging the mourners as they made their way out of the cemetery.

"What are you doing here?" I said as he reached the bench.

"Same as you, probably. Hiding."

I stared up at him, surprised. How did he know? Was it that obvious, or had he seen me run in?

"Is it your dad?" I said. "Is he drunk again?"

He didn't speak straight away. He was staring at the one or two people who'd hung back by the new grave. "It's the anniversary of my mum's death," he said when they'd turned to go. "She died two years ago today." He paused as if he was searching for the right words. "My dad's not coping too well, if you get what I mean."

I nodded, not sure what to say. There didn't seem to be anything that could make it better.

"How about you?" I said in the end. "Are you coping?"

His face crumpled suddenly and he looked away.

"I'm coping better than he is," he said, his voice thick. "Thanks for asking."

We sat in the cemetery for ages. I told Kieran about Dad and Sharon and the girl from school, and how I'd seen them all in the cafe on Saturday. "I'm pretty sure my dad and Sharon are together. I think he was about to tell me just now, but then his phone rang and I just took off…"

Kieran sighed. "Why do grown-ups always make everything so complicated?" he said. He sounded about a hundred years old.

We chatted a bit more and then Mum rang to say she wanted me home.

"Great rounder by the way," said Kieran as I got up to leave.

I wondered what he meant for a minute; I'd forgotten all about it. "Oh that. You didn't even see…"

"Of course I did, or why would I say it? I used to be on the rounders team at my primary school so I know what I'm talking about."

"*You* were in the rounders team?"

"Don't look so surprised. They used to call me The Bullet because the ball flew across the field like a bullet whenever I hit it."

I smiled. It was a nice image. "You should come to rounders club some time," I said. "Show everyone how good you are."

"You are joking, aren't you?"

"No, I'm dead serious. I didn't want to go either when Gemma first suggested it."

"I don't *do* clubs at school," he said. "No one would want me there anyway."

"Scared I might be better than you?" I teased.

He stood up to face me. "Is that a challenge, Maddie Wilkins?"

"Yes that *is* a challenge, Kieran *The Bullet* Black. So do you accept or are you too chicken?"

He didn't answer but he smiled. A proper smile. It changed his face completely – as if someone had switched the lights back on after a very long time.

I had no idea what would happen when I got back, or whether Dad would be there waiting to talk to me. I tried to sneak in as quietly as I could, but Mum called me into the kitchen and asked me to lay the table as if nothing had happened. She'd made my favourite dinner – lasagne with garlic bread – and as soon as I smelled it in the oven, I realized how hungry I was.

She didn't mention Dad while we were eating, except to tell me he'd be home late. I guess she didn't want to say anything in front of Charlie. He had his football trial coming up and was attempting to discuss tactics with us.

"Rory's great up front," he was saying, "everyone knows that, but someone has to be there to feed the ball in otherwise what's the point?"

Mum and I both shrugged. Neither of us had a clue about football.

"The others don't realize that feeding the ball in is just as important as scoring, isn't it, Mum?"

"Course," Mum murmured, glancing at me across the table.

There was so much to say. So much we *needed* to say and none of it had anything to do with Charlie and his football trials. If only I had the courage to face up to it. She waited until tea was finished and he was outside practising. As soon as she heard the familiar thud of the ball against the wall she said, "What happened after rounders, Maddie? Dad said you ran off and that you were very upset but he wasn't sure why."

I started to stack the dirty plates up, stalling. "It was nothing really," I said after a bit. "He was about to tell me something and then his phone rang and apparently it was so important he had to take it…" It was difficult to keep the bitterness out of my voice. I was so sick of all the lies, all the pretending. Mum came up behind me and turned me round to face her.

"I know this is hard for you, Mads, but the phone call *was* important; it's all tied up with what he was going to tell you. I can see you're upset and anxious but he couldn't help it, he had to go…"

"So where was Dad on Saturday then?" I interrupted. My heart started to thump. I'd said it now; it was too late to change my mind.

"What do you mean?" said Mum without missing a beat. "He took Charlie to the park for a big training session, remember? They were there for hours…"

"I know, but in the morning, *before* that?"

Mum frowned. Her eyes were fixed on my face. "He went into town," she said. "He had a meeting with someone. We went together, just after you left to meet up with Gemma."

I couldn't believe it. She was lying. Covering for him. Why would she do that? Why would she say she was *with* him? It didn't make sense.

"I don't understand…" I said, more confused than ever. "I just want to know what's going on with Dad and Sharon, Mum. I feel…I feel like I'm losing him…"

"You are *not* losing him, Mads. This isn't even about Dad and Sharon, not really. Look, I want you to come home straight after school tomorrow, no hanging around with Gemma or at the cemetery. Dad will be here and we'll have a proper talk, the three of us together. I can see you're upset, and this has gone on far too long, but I really don't want you to worry. Everything is going to be okay, I promise."

* * *

I sneaked out early the next morning. I wanted to speak to Vivian before the others got there. I still felt a bit funny about seeing her with that Year Seven boy straight after I'd confided in her, but I'd hardly slept all night worrying about what Dad was going to say, trying to piece it all together: Sharon, the woman in the cemetery, the note, the girl with the ponytail.

It was over four weeks since Sharon first called, nearly a month since Dad met up with her that night. I'd been so certain he'd started having a relationship with her, that he was lying to us, that him and Mum were splitting up, but suddenly I wasn't so sure. Maybe I'd got it all wrong. Maybe she'd got in touch with Dad for some completely different reason. Nan used to say I was brilliant at getting the wrong end of the stick – adding two and two together and getting five.

The door to the Blue Room was open slightly as I came up the corridor. I could hear voices. It was Mrs Palmer talking to Vivian. "You won't be having Kieran today, I'm afraid," she was saying.

My stomach clenched up. I got as close to the door as I could, straining to hear. Something was wrong. I could feel it in my gut.

"I thought I'd better come and tell you myself," Mrs Palmer went on. "Kieran was taken to hospital by ambulance late last night."

21

Coming Face-to-Face

I just about got out of the way as the door swung open and Mrs Palmer came out.

"Oh goodness, Maddie, you gave me a fright! I hope I didn't hurt you."

"No, I'm fine," I said. She began to walk past, her heels clicking down the corridor. "Mrs Palmer!" I called out, before I could lose my nerve. She turned back towards me, smiling. "Um…I heard what you said about Kieran just now. I wasn't eavesdropping or anything I was just standing right outside. Is he okay?"

"I understand he's your friend, Maddie, and that it's worrying," she said gently. "But apart from the fact that he was taken to Hadley General last night, I'm afraid I don't know much else about it at the moment."

It sounded weird, hearing her say Kieran was my friend. Kieran Black, who used to go out of his way to torment me – but she was right, he was my friend, and I honestly couldn't bear it if anything had happened to him. I turned around slowly and trailed into the Blue Room, a plan already forming in my head. I had to get up to the hospital – to show him that someone cared.

"Morning, Maddie," said Vivian. She held the pad out to me but I shook my head; I didn't have time to draw today or waste my time doodling.

"I'm really worried about Kieran," I blurted out. "I overheard what Mrs Palmer said and I need to find out if he's okay. And that's not all. I saw my dad in a cafe with this woman; I'd seen her before in the cemetery, by my nan's grave, and once more, here at school, and there was a girl with them, about my age, a bit older. Then a few days later I saw the girl again. She was hanging round my locker, waiting for me…"

"Waiting for you?" said Vivian frowning. "What do you mean? Did you speak to her?"

I shook my head, sinking down into the nearest chair. "As soon as she saw me she took off, as if she was scared, or she'd done something wrong."

Vivian was quiet for a moment. "Look, I'm worried about Kieran as well," she said slowly. "Maybe I could try to ring the hospital in a bit. As far as your family goes, and this girl, I really think you should talk to your dad. Does he know you saw him in the cafe?"

I shook my head. "I've only told Kieran and my best friend Gemma. I'm finding it really difficult to talk to my dad at the moment. He's being so secretive. Apparently we're going to have this big family talk later this afternoon but I'm dreading it. It's like I want to know, but I'm scared of knowing at the same time…"

"Listen to me, Maddie, you need to talk to your dad, or if you can't manage that, then talk to your mum. Of course it's scary, there's obviously something going on, but you'll feel so much better once it's all out in the open…"

"I know you're right and I don't want to run away any more. I just find it so difficult…"

Vivian reached out to touch my arm. "Look, if it makes it any easier, I could talk to Mrs Palmer after the session and set up a meeting with your parents here, maybe for tomorrow? I'd be happy to do that if you think it would help."

I nodded, relieved. Maybe I'd been wrong about Vivian not caring after all. Just at that moment Sally-Ann came rushing in. "Sorry I'm a bit late," she said. "What have I missed?"

I tuned out as they chatted. A meeting with Mum and Dad *and* Vivian. I was still frightened, but Vivian was right; knowing had to be better than not knowing, however awful the truth turned out to be. And it would be so much easier if Vivian was actually there when Mum and Dad told me…

"Did you hear what I was saying, Maddie?" Sally-Ann waved her hand in front of my face. "I told my mum how I was feeling about her new boyfriend – how I was worried she didn't want me around any more, and she was really shocked. She said she had no idea; that I always acted like I couldn't care less when he came over…"

"So was your mum nice about it?" I asked, thinking of Dad.

Sally-Ann nodded. "Really nice. She said I had nothing to worry about, that I'd *always* come first, no matter what."

I hung back at the end of the session to talk to Vivian about the meeting. She said she'd speak to Mrs Palmer as soon as she could and that one of them would let me know what was going on later. She said she appreciated me confiding in her, that it was extremely brave. I shook my head, confused. It's not as if I'd confronted Dad, or talked to Mum, or done anything really.

Gemma was waiting for me by my locker.

"Is everything okay?" she said. "Where were you this morning? What happened with your dad?"

"I'm sorry; I had to come in early to talk to Vivian. She's going to set up a meeting with my parents." I hesitated. "Um, to be honest, Gemma, I'm more worried about Kieran at the moment."

"Kieran *Black*?"

"Yes, Kieran *Black*, and before you freak out or anything, just listen, *please*!"

I told her what I'd overheard before the session, and about Kieran's mum dying and what happened with his dad in the cemetery. She might not like Kieran but I knew I could trust her. Her eyes were so huge behind her glasses they practically filled her entire face.

"I can't believe it. 'No more secrets', you said! All this stuff has been going on and you haven't said a word!"

"I know, I'm sorry, I should've told you, but I wasn't sure if Kieran would want people to know about his mum and you have to *swear* not to say anything to anyone. Anyway, listen, I need to go to the hospital straight after school, just to make sure he's okay, and I really want you to come with me." I kept my eyes fixed on her face, praying she'd say yes, but she stared back at me as if I'd asked her to fly to the moon.

"You're joking, aren't you? That's totally bonkers, Maddie. We won't know what ward he's on and even if we find him, they won't let us actually *see him*, not unless we're relatives, and—"

"We'll make something up," I cut in, before she could come up with any other reasons. "We'll work it out on the way. Please, Gemma, I'm begging you."

She rolled her eyes, groaning. "Okay, okay, I'll come, but I still think you're mad."

It doesn't take long to get to Hadley General; it's about twenty minutes out of town by bus – the same hospital Nan was in when she had her stroke. I'll never forget the day I went to visit. She'd already been in hospital for nearly a week, but I'd been too scared to visit. By the time I plucked up the courage to go she'd caught the infection and taken a turn for the worse.

Mum tried to warn me in the lift before we got up to the ward, but it was even worse than I was expecting. She looked too small for a start, as if they'd put her in the washing machine and shrunk her. Her face was saggy, drooping down on one side, and there was a line of dribble coming out of her mouth.

I edged towards the bed and told her it was me, that I'd come to visit, that I was sorry it had taken so long. I begged and pleaded with her to wake up. I kept saying, *it's me, Nan, it's me, Maddie*, over and over, but it was too late. She didn't move. She couldn't even hear me. She'd slipped into a coma that morning and she never woke up again. Mum had to drag me away in the end, out of the ward and back down in the lift.

I couldn't help wishing Mum was with us now; she'd know what to do for the best. I texted her to say I was going back to Gemma's and that I'd be home before dinner. I knew she'd be cross, she was expecting me straight home for the Big Talk, but I couldn't let myself worry about that until I'd seen Kieran and made sure he was okay.

We sat at the top of the bus, chatting. Gemma wanted to know all about Kieran and his mum and dad. She said she felt bad not knowing his mum had died – that if people knew they'd understand why he was in trouble all the time. I tried to stay as calm as I could as the bus trundled along, but I had no idea what we were going to find when we got to the hospital – or if they'd even agree to let us see him.

There was a crowd of people just outside the main entrance, most of them smoking or on their phones. We weaved our way through and went over to the main reception desk.

"We've come to visit Kieran Black," I said, trying to sound more confident than I was feeling. "He was brought in last night…"

The receptionist tapped something into her computer and then looked up, her face bored, as if she'd already dealt with a million people that day. "You'll find him in Meadow Ward on the third floor. The lifts are straight ahead on the right-hand side."

We hurried down the corridor before she could say anything else.

"I honestly didn't think it would be as easy as that," I said, relieved but panicking at the same time. "What are we going to do when we get up there? What if they're suspicious? It might not even be visiting time."

I'd been so desperate to come, but now we were here I wasn't so sure. Gemma was right, I wasn't related to Kieran. I had no idea why he was here or how ill he was. It suddenly felt as if I was poking my nose into something far too private. I didn't say a word in the lift but as the doors slid opened I reached for Gemma's hand and she squeezed it tight.

"I hate hospitals," I said, wishing we could go. "I've always hated them ever since Charlie was a baby – and then coming here when my nan was ill…I don't think I can do it…"

"I don't feel brilliant either," she whispered. "The last time I was at hospital was when my mum had her scan. But we're here now, Mads."

The first thing that hit me was the smell. It was a mixture of sick and disinfectant. Exactly the same smell as when I came to visit Nan. I had to breathe through my mouth to stop myself from retching. All the memories came crowding back. I had an overwhelming urge to run, to get as far away as I could.

We made our way over to another desk in the middle of the ward. There was a massive whiteboard behind it listing all the patients. I scanned it for Kieran's name but it was difficult to read the scribbled writing. I cleared my throat and one of the nurses looked up from her computer.

"Yes, can I help you, girls?"

"We've come to see Kieran Black," I said. "He was… um…he was brought in last night."

The nurse stared at me for what seemed like the longest time and then turned to the nurse next to her. They got up and moved to the side talking in hushed voices.

"Something's happened to him," I said to Gemma. "I'm sure of it."

She reached for my hand, squeezing it even tighter. The first nurse came back over, sitting down again before she spoke.

"Are you related to Kieran?" she asked. "Are you here with anyone else? Mum or Dad?"

I shook my head. "We're friends from school. We just wanted to make sure he was okay."

"Well the thing is, girls, he's not actually here any more," she said. "He was discharged this morning…" She trailed off.

"So he's okay then?" said Gemma.

"Yes, he's fine," she said firmly. "I'm sure he'll back at school in no time at all."

She looked at her computer screen, tapping a few keys. The conversation was over as far as she was concerned, but I still had a million questions.

"Come on," said Gemma. "At least you know he's okay." She pulled me away from the desk and we trailed out of the ward.

"I still think something's wrong," I said, as we waited for the lift. "I wish I knew why they brought him here in the first place."

"I know, but they were never going to tell us. That sort

of stuff is confidential, even if it's something as simple as a throat infection or chickenpox."

"Yeah, but you don't get taken to hospital in an ambulance in the middle of the night for a throat infection. What if his dad did something to him? Hurt him in some way? Do you think I should go back and ask?"

Gemma shook her head. "Seriously, Maddie, there's no point. They won't tell you, and anyway, look, the lift's here now."

The light at the side of the lift flashed yellow as the doors began to slide open. There was a girl inside. She was wearing a Church Vale uniform, her brown hair tied up in a ponytail. She looked up, took a step towards us and then froze.

It was her.

The girl from school.

The girl I'd seen in the cafe with Dad.

22

Jasmine

"What are you doing here?" she said, as if she knew me. "What's happened?"

I stared at her, trying to understand.

"Don't mess around, Maddie!" Her voice rose in panic. "Come on, I'm not joking! Just *tell* me!"

"W…what do you mean?" I stuttered. "Who are you? W…we just came to see Kieran Black, but he was discharged this morning."

She stepped out of the lift, relief flooding her face. She was really pretty – honey-brown eyes, shiny sun-streaked hair.

"Is that true?" she said turning to Gemma. "Is that why you're here?"

Gemma nodded. She seemed as shocked as me. "We came here to see Kieran, but what are *you* doing here, Jasmine?"

"*Jasmine?*" I said, more confused than ever. How on earth did Gemma know her name?

"Look I've got to go," she muttered, pushing past us. "I'm sorry."

"Stop! Wait a minute!" I grabbed for her arm but I was too slow. "What's going on? I need to talk to you."

She paused for a moment, turning back.

"I know it's you," I said, desperate to find out the truth. "I saw you with my dad in the cafe last Saturday and you were hanging about by my locker…"

The girl took a step towards me, her eyes filling with tears. There was nothing frightening about her close-up. She looked as scared as I was feeling, and not only that, she looked familiar. Not just familiar because I'd seen her before; familiar in a different way, as if I already knew her.

"You'll have to ask your dad," she said. "Ask him and he'll tell you everything. But I can't stop now. I'm *really* sorry, Maddie, I've got to go."

She took off down the corridor, in the opposite direction to Meadow Ward, her ponytail swinging behind her. I stood there watching her until she disappeared through another set of double doors. For a minute it was like I'd imagined the whole thing. Like I was stuck in a bad dream and nothing that had just happened was real.

"Oh my god," said Gemma. "What was all that about?"

"How do you know her?" I said. "I mean, I recognize her from the cafe and from school, but how do you actually know her *name?*"

"She's in maths club," said Gemma. "She's in Year Ten, but it's not just for Year Eights, remember? I think she only started at Church Vale this term. She's really nice, Maddie, and super-smart."

"I don't believe it. You actually knew who she was all along. Why do you think she was so freaked out when she saw me? It's obviously got nothing to do with Kieran... she looked so frightened."

Gemma shrugged. "I have no idea, Mads. You *really* need to talk to your dad."

"I know," I said quietly. "I'm going to."

I sent Dad a text from the bus. I said I was on my way home and we needed to talk. I couldn't wait until Vivian organized a meeting. I had a right to know what was going on – to find out why *Jasmine* seemed to be more clued up than me.

The nearer we got to home, the more I began to panic. I was itching to reach into my bag for my ribbon but I felt awkward with Gemma sitting next to me. I knew she wouldn't care but it was still embarrassing. I tried breathing as slowly as I could, doing my best to calm myself down without it.

"Are you okay?" said Gemma.

I nodded, grateful she was there. She'd been amazing, agreeing to come with me after what happened with her mum. She began to tell me about a time she'd been rushed to hospital with a virus when she was six. She said she didn't remember much about it, just that she loved the food, especially the lasagne.

"My mum was so upset. Seriously, Maddie, she made lasagne for weeks after that, desperate to prove she could do it better than the hospital! I'm not kidding you, she made it so many times I can't stand it any more. To be honest I'd rather eat my own arm than a plate of lasagne." She cuddled up to me, resting her head on my shoulder. "Try not to worry, Mads. I'm sure it'll all be okay once you talk to your mum and dad."

Dad must've called Mum as soon as he got my text. She was waiting for me on the doorstep, her phone clutched in her hand. "What's going on?" she said. "Where have you been?"

"I was up at Hadley General," I said. "I went to see Kieran but he'd already been discharged."

"What are you talking about?" she said, her face clouding with confusion. "I thought you said you were going over to Gemma's, and then I had this call from Mrs Palmer about a meeting, and your dad's just called to say he's on his way home, that you texted him. What's going on, Maddie? What's it got to do with Kieran?"

"It hasn't really got anything to do with Kieran," I said, as she led me through to the kitchen. "Well it has, but I'll tell you about that later." I felt a bit dizzy, as if the floor was tilting beneath me, as if after today, after the next *hour*, nothing would ever be the same again.

"Start at the beginning," said Mum gently. "Mrs Palmer said she wanted to arrange a meeting with Vivian…"

"Look, I'll tell you everything when Dad gets here. Vivian suggested meeting together but we don't need to now. Dad is coming, isn't he?"

Mum nodded, getting up to flip the switch on the kettle. "He said he'd be here as soon as he could. He's just finishing a job. He was planning to be here when you got back from school but he got held up. Charlie's gone back to Rory's. I thought it would be better if we talked to you first."

She poured us both a cup of tea, adding loads of sugar

to mine, almost as if she could sense I'd had a shock at the hospital. A moment later, just as she sat back down, we heard Dad's van pull up outside. "That'll be him," she said, jumping up again. "Stay in here for a minute, Mads, I won't be long."

I could hear them in the hall, whispering. It was impossible to make out what they were saying, but when they came in Mum seemed to be angry. "So you know about Jasmine!" she blurted out, before I could say hi to Dad or anything. I was so confused – and then I guessed what must have happened: Jasmine must have called Dad straight after she saw us in the hospital. Warned him that we'd come face-to-face.

"Yes...sort of...I mean, I know she met up with Dad on Saturday, I saw her in the cafe, and I know she goes to Church Vale, but I don't who she is...I don't actually *know* anything."

"I didn't want you to find out like this," said Mum. "I said to Dad right from the start that we had to be careful about telling you; that it would be difficult for you to cope with another big change."

"I know, I heard you on the phone to Aunty Hat, but I still don't know what you're talking about, what the big change *is*..." I pushed my chair back, standing up to face them. "There's so much I don't understand, I really wish you'd tell me. The woman in the cemetery? Sharon? *Jasmine?* I mean how come she knows who I am? Who *is* she?"

"Oh, sweetheart." Dad held his arms out towards me but I backed away.

"Don't!" I said. "I don't want you to hug me and tell me it's all going to be okay when it's not. I don't want you to lie or make things up, or treat me like a little girl. I'm sick of it, Dad. I just want to know the truth."

"We were only trying to protect you, Maddie," said Mum. "We should've told you sooner but we were *scared*, there was so much going on…"

"Protect me from *what*? Scared to tell me *what*?"

My breath was coming really fast now; I pressed my hands to my chest, looking from Dad to Mum and back to Dad. Everything in me was screaming *run away*, but I forced myself to stay where I was. Dad's face began to crumple. I'd never seen him cry before apart from that night when he came back from meeting Sharon and his eyes were red. But this was worse. Tears were actually streaming down his face. It was horrible.

"I didn't know until a few weeks ago myself," he said, choking on the words. "I had no idea. It was like a bolt from the blue…"

"*What* was a bolt from the blue? Just tell me!"

"She's my daughter, Maddie." Dad shook his head slightly as if he couldn't believe it himself. "Jasmine is my daughter."

23

Pushed Out

No one moved. It was as if Dad's words had put a bad spell on all three of us. How could Jasmine be his daughter? I was his daughter. His eyes were fixed on mine, watching to see how I'd react. I waited for him to tell me it wasn't true. I waited for him to say it was all a mistake or some kind of stupid joke, but I knew Dad would never joke about something so serious. And anyway I could see in his eyes that it was true.

It was even worse than I'd imagined. I never thought for a moment that the girl in the cafe was *related* to Dad. How could you have a daughter and not know about her? It didn't make any sense. I opened my mouth to ask him and then closed it again.

Dad began to speak in a soft voice. "I know this is a shock for you, Maddie. It was a shock for me too when I found out, and for Mum."

I glanced at Mum. She nodded, giving me a shaky smile.

"It's a long story," Dad went on, "and I'm sure you've got lots of questions. Why don't we all sit down at the table and I'll try to explain."

Mum moved first. "Come on, Maddie, Dad's right, we need to talk."

I still felt like running, even more than before, to shut myself in my room and hide under my covers with my ribbon. But at the same time I could hear Vivian telling Kieran how brave he was to stay when things got tough. It's not as if running away or refusing to listen would make Jasmine disappear. I sat down at the table as if I was in a trance.

"Jasmine's mum, Sharon, was my girlfriend," said Dad when we were all sitting down. "We were together for about three years. We broke up just before I met your mum." He reached out to take Mum's hand. "I didn't see her again after we broke up. It was…well…to be honest, it wasn't a very good ending. She thought I'd been seeing Mum behind her back. It turned bitter, a lot of unpleasant things were said, and then shortly afterwards she moved away."

"But she was pregnant," said Mum, taking over. "She didn't tell Dad, so he had no idea."

It was a relief to see them holding hands. It helped to ease the knot in my stomach that had been growing bigger by the minute.

"I had no idea," Dad carried on. "It was a total shock. Imagine finding out you've got a fifteen-year-old daughter…"

"You're not explaining properly," I said. "How did you find out?"

Dad took a breath. "Well, you kind of know that bit of the story," he said. "Sharon called up and said she'd moved back to the area; she wanted to meet up with me to discuss something."

"That night when you came back and your eyes were red and puffy…" I said, thinking back. "Did she tell you about Jasmine in the pub? Is that why you were upset?"

"Partly," said Dad, nodding. "She did tell me about Jasmine, but it wasn't just that…"

"I still don't understand," I whispered. "Why did she get in touch with you after so many years? Why did she change her mind about you meeting Jasmine?"

Mum and Dad glanced at each other.

"It's because Sharon's ill," said Dad, staring down at the table. "She's very ill. They're not sure she's going to get better. She's been in and out of hospital having treatment. That's partly why it's taken us so long to tell you…"

I felt like I'd been kicked in the stomach. I couldn't catch my breath for a minute. It was so sad, for Sharon *and* Jasmine. "That's so awful."

"Yes, and that's why Jasmine was at the hospital today," Dad went on. "Why she was so scared when she saw you. She thought something had happened to her mum…"

"But how did she know it was me?"

"She's seen photos of you, sweetheart. Some on my phone and the ones I got from the attic that day…" Dad paused for a moment, closing his eyes. "The reason Sharon got in touch with me after all these years was because she didn't want Jasmine to be left alone without any family…if the worst happened and it came to that. Sharon's an only child and her parents died a long time ago. There are no aunts or uncles or cousins. She had to think about what would happen if she couldn't look after Jasmine any more.

"They've rented a flat near the hospital and a close friend of Sharon's has moved in to look after Jasmine, but she can't always be there, what with work and everything, so I've been helping out as much as I can as well."

"I saw you together in the cafe," I said, staring down at my hands. "I was outside with Gemma and I saw you through the window."

"Oh god, Maddie. I didn't know. We didn't see you. I can't believe you've been carrying this around since then…"

"But Sharon was there too," I said. "I saw her, and I saw her at the cemetery and up at school. How come she's not in hospital if she's so ill? It doesn't make any sense."

"We'd just come from the hospital," said Dad. "She had to have some more tests before she was re-admitted for her next course of treatment. That's why I kept answering my phone when we were together. I was worried it was bad news. I honestly didn't mean to be so secretive, sweetheart, but I needed some time to get my head round everything myself before I told you and Charlie…"

He trailed off, looking at Mum for help.

"I was in the cafe as well," said Mum quietly. "I must've been in the loo when you were outside with Gemma. I was hiding in there, trying to pluck up the courage to come out and meet Jasmine and Sharon for the first time.

You're not the only who gets anxious, Mads," she added, giving me a strained smile. "I don't think I'd ever been so scared in my life!"

"Jasmine really wants to meet you too," said Dad. "And Charlie of course. She's so excited to meet you both." His eyes were kind of glowing as if he could already imagine us all together – one big happy family. "I know it's a lot to take in, Maddie, but Jasmine's not just my daughter; she's also your sister."

The words hung in the air between us. I could almost see them. *She's also your sister.* As if I was supposed to be pleased. I looked away, a shot of acid curdling my stomach. And then suddenly I realized why there was something familiar about Jasmine, why I felt as if I already knew her. It was because she looked exactly like Dad: the same dark-brown eyes, the same mouth, the same open face.

It was too much. I couldn't bear it. I didn't want Dad to have another daughter. *I* was his daughter. I jumped up from the table.

"I don't want to meet her!" I said. "I hate her. I wish she'd go back to wherever it was she came from and leave us alone. I don't want a new sister." I couldn't hold the tears back any longer. "I hate Jasmine," I sobbed. "I hate her. I hate her. *I hate her.*"

Mum jumped up and rushed over to put her arms round me.

"It's okay," she said. "Come on, Maddie, it's okay. I know it's difficult but it doesn't change Dad's feelings for you, or Charlie."

I pushed her away. "What do you mean? Of course it does. It changes everything. I don't want to see her *or* Dad." I swung round to face him. "You already spend more time with her than you do with us, rushing off every minute, out every night. It's obvious how you really feel, where you *really* want to be!"

I tore out of the kitchen and up to my room. I felt so betrayed, rejected, as if someone had reached into my chest and torn my heart into tiny little pieces. I pulled my ribbon out from my bag and wrapped it around my hand, but it didn't make the pain go away.

Dad didn't need me any more. He had Jasmine now.

I don't know how long I lay there. I heard Charlie come home at some point and tried to imagine his face as Mum and Dad told him – how awful he'd feel. At least I understood now why they'd been so scared to tell me. Dad couldn't have *two* families. What was he planning to do? Spend half the time with us and half the time with Jasmine and Sharon?

"Maddie?" The door opened a crack. It was Charlie. "Maddie, can I come in?"

He came in anyway before I could answer, pushing the door open and then standing there, rooted to the spot, as if he wasn't sure what to do next. He was wearing his school shorts and T-shirt, his knees covered in mud.

"Have they told you?" I said, sitting up and patting the side of the bed.

He nodded, but he didn't come over. "You look terrible, Mads. What's happened to your eyes?"

"Nothing's happened to them, they're just puffy because I've been crying. How was school?"

"We played football at playtime and my team won," he said. "I set up the first goal. So what do you think about Jasmine then?"

"I hate her," I said.

"Me too," he said, but he didn't sound sure. He scuffed the floor with his foot, looking round my room as if he might find the right answer up on the wall somewhere. "I'm going out in the garden," he muttered in the end. "See you."

Mum came up a bit later. She came straight over to my bed and sat down, pulling me towards her.

"What are we going to do?" I said, leaning into her. "What's going to happen?"

She stroked my hair for a while and then pulled back from me, holding my shoulders and looking directly into my eyes.

"You don't really have to do anything at the moment, Maddie. We understand what a massive shock this has been for you…"

"So you're not going to make me meet her or anything?"

"No of course not, there's no rush for that at all…" She pulled me close again. "I mean eventually Jasmine *is* going to be part of our family, but we'll do it at your pace…"

I couldn't believe it. "No!" I said, twisting away. "She isn't. How can you say that?"

Mum took hold of my shoulders again. "Listen to me, sweetheart. I understand how you feel, how much you're hurting right now. I'm not suggesting we all start playing happy families and I certainly don't expect you to welcome her with open arms, but…"

I put my hands over my ears, shaking my head. "I'll never welcome her. Never! I don't care what you say."

Mum pulled my hands away gently, squeezing them tight. "Jasmine is going through a terrible time, sweetheart. You wouldn't expect your dad to turn his back on her. She's a part of him. She's part of you too, and Charlie."

"But I don't want a new sister," I whispered. "I just

want my dad back. I don't even know if he loves me any more."

"Maddie Wilkins! Your father adores you. He'd do *anything* for you and Charlie. You're his life. I know it's scary – probably the scariest thing that's ever happened to you. And I know you won't believe me, not for a while anyway, but remember what your nan always used to say, how sometimes the scariest things turn out to be the best."

I turned to face the wall, gathering my ribbon into my hand. Nan *did* used to say that. I remember her saying it the night before I started Church Vale. I was struggling to get to sleep, worried about making new friends and fitting in. Scared I'd get lost on my way to class, or have no one to eat my lunch with.

But coping with your first day at secondary school isn't really the same as finding out your dad's got a brand-new daughter.

24
A Message
From Kieran

I told Gemma about Jasmine as soon as I got to school
the next morning. It felt strange saying it out loud,
like admitting to myself that it was really true. I so wanted
her to say, *Oh no, that's awful, what are you going to do?*
I was desperate for her to understand how I was feeling,
but she grabbed my arm, pulling me round to face her,
her eyes lit up like a Christmas tree.

"Your *sister*?" she breathed. "No way! That's *incredible*,
Maddie. It's just…oh my god…your *sister*…you are *so*
lucky!"

"Lucky!" I said, pulling my arm away. "What are you
talking about? There's nothing *lucky* about it!"

She shrank back, as if I'd hit her. "Sorry, I didn't mean to say the wrong thing…I've just always wanted a sister… you know I have…and, well, Jasmine's so nice…"

"No she's not! You don't even know her… just because she goes to maths club!"

"I know, I know, I just meant—"

"It doesn't matter," I snapped, cutting her off. "I've got to go anyway. I need to find out if Kieran's okay."

I rushed off down the corridor before she could say anything else. I felt awful, especially since she'd told me about her mum being pregnant and losing the baby, but how would she like it if her dad suddenly announced that he had a new daughter? I bet she wouldn't be so keen, even if it was someone as *nice* as Jasmine was supposed to be.

I couldn't stop thinking about Jasmine and Dad together. They were probably growing closer every day, hanging out, bonding, making up for lost time. I felt pushed out, as if I'd been replaced. Jasmine was new and exciting. How was I supposed to compete with that?

I got to the Blue Room just before registration. I wasn't even sure if Vivian would be there, but it had to be worth a try. I was only planning to ask her about Kieran, but standing there, knocking on the door, I was suddenly desperate to tell her everything. About the hospital, and seeing Jasmine there, and finding out. At least *she'd* understand how frightened I was feeling.

"Maddie?"

I swung round. It was Mrs Palmer, striding up the corridor towards me.

"Is everything okay? Vivian isn't due in until eleven today. You'd better hurry to registration or you'll be late."

There was still no sign of Kieran when I got to class and he didn't show up for any morning lessons. I just needed to see him, to make sure he was okay. I tried to remember the way his face changed when I'd challenged him to join rounders club. The way it lit up suddenly. It was hard to believe it was only two days ago, so much had happened since then.

Gemma went out of her way to avoid me, sitting as far away from me as she could in class. I tried to say sorry for snapping but she kept rushing off, sweeping straight past me as if we were strangers. Going from class to class by myself was a nightmare – I was terrified I might bump into Jasmine, even more so than before. I seriously had no idea what I'd do if we came face-to-face.

I managed to survive until lunch, hurrying down corridors, keeping my head down, doing my best to blend in with the crowd, and then just when I was least expecting it, it happened. I'd gone back to the Blue Room to talk to Vivian – my hand was literally on the doorknob – when the door swung open and Jasmine walked out.

"*Maddie!*"

I stumbled back, a million thoughts flooding my head. What was she doing in the Blue Room? Why was she with Vivian? Did that mean Vivian knew about us being sisters? Had she been hiding it from me? Keeping secrets like everyone else?

Jasmine reached her arm out to steady me. "Are you okay? I didn't mean to startle you."

I just stood there staring at her.

"Please, Maddie, say something."

I didn't know what to do. My brain was screaming at me to run but my legs had turned to jelly. Seeing her close up again was even more shocking than yesterday at the hospital. She was so tall and pretty, so like Dad. I pushed past her into the Blue Room. Vivian was standing just inside the door and I could see from her face that none of this was a surprise. She must've known all along.

"I'm going to talk to Maddie now," she said to Jasmine. "I'll see you next time, okay?" She closed the door gently and turned to face me. "Why don't you come and sit down? Would you like a glass of water?"

I shook my head, sinking down into the nearest chair. "How long have you known? Has it been some big joke?

Have you all been laughing at me behind my back?"

Vivian sat down opposite me, leaning forward. "I've been seeing Jasmine for a number of weeks, helping her settle into school and to cope with her mum's illness, but I only realized she was related to you yesterday when we spoke. Jasmine had mentioned that she had a new sister, but it was only at that point that I put two and two together."

"How do I know you're telling me the truth?" I said, not quite able to meet her eye. "Everyone's been keeping secrets – my mum and dad, Sharon, Jasmine. How do I *know* you've only just found out?"

"You'll have to trust me, Maddie. I can't talk to you about my sessions with Jasmine, it wouldn't be right, but if I'd known you were related to each other before yesterday I would've stopped my sessions with both of you immediately. There would've been a conflict of interests. Do you know what that means?"

I shrugged, desperately wanting to believe her, but at the same time certain she was lying.

"Basically it means that from a professional point of view, it wouldn't have been right for me to carry on my sessions with you *or* Jasmine." She paused for a moment. "And I certainly won't be able to now. Not unless you agree to see me together."

My head snapped up. "What do you mean, *together*?"

"Well, I think you and Jasmine are both going to need some help coming to terms with what's happened, the fact that you're related, that you've been unexpectedly thrown together, but the only way I can see either of you again is if you agree to have a joint session."

"No way!" I said, wrapping my arms around my body. "I'm not sitting in here with her. I don't believe this! She's taken my dad away from me, and now she's taking you away from me as well!"

"No one's taking your dad away from you, Maddie," she said gently. "How do you think he might be feeling, finding out about Jasmine after so many years? This is an extremely difficult situation for all of you…"

"I thought you'd understand," I said, trying not to cry. "I thought out of *everyone*, you'd realize how frightened I am."

She reached across the table for my hand but I shrank back. "I do understand, Maddie. Of course you're frightened. When you first came to see me you were struggling to come to terms with losing your nan and now everything's changing again. But Jasmine's facing lots of changes as well, and I honestly think you could help each other."

My tummy clenched up. I knew she was right, that Jasmine was going through a terrible ordeal, much worse than anything I'd been through, but I couldn't help how I was feeling.

"It's not the same," I said lamely. "I wouldn't even know *how* to help her."

Vivian nodded. "No, of course it's not the same," she said, "that's not what I meant. Just that you're both dealing with difficult feelings and you're both frightened." She paused for a moment, reaching in her bag for her diary. "I'm going to ask Jasmine to come here on Monday at nine. I'll set aside an hour and ask Mrs Palmer to excuse you from your first class. I really hope you'll come too, Maddie."

"I won't," I muttered. "I don't want to, and I won't change my mind."

I got up from the table and trailed over to the door. Why couldn't I carry on my normal sessions with Kieran and Sally-Ann? I didn't want to come to some special session with Jasmine. I didn't want to do things differently.

"Just think about it," said Vivian as I was leaving. "Oh and Maddie, I thought you might like to know. Kieran's gone to stay with his aunt and uncle for a while, but we're hoping he'll be back at school on Monday."

I rushed off, relieved that Kieran was okay, but too upset about everything else to ask Vivian what had actually happened to him. I avoided the cafeteria and spent the rest of the lunch hour in the library. I didn't feel like eating anyway. I hid away at the back pretending to read, thinking about Jasmine and Vivian and meeting up together, wondering how things had gone so wrong. How I'd managed to lose everything.

The more I thought about it the smaller I felt, as if I'd let everyone down: Mum and Dad and Vivian and Gemma. Even Jasmine and Sharon.

Gemma went out of her way to avoid me all afternoon. I was dying to talk to her, to tell her how sorry I was for snapping. I tried catching her eye a few times during the afternoon but it was obvious she didn't want to speak to me. I couldn't believe I'd been so insensitive. Of course she thought I was lucky to have a sister after what happened with her mum and the baby.

It was unbearably hot as I made my way down Banner Road at the end of the day, the sort of weather that drags you down. My shirt was stuck to my back and my bag felt too heavy. I trailed through the cemetery, stopping by Nan's grave. I couldn't face going home to an empty house. I couldn't face anything.

I tried to imagine what Nan would think about Dad having another daughter – what advice she might give me. Jasmine was her granddaughter too, but she'd never know that now. Maybe that was why Sharon left a note saying sorry. Sorry for keeping Jasmine away from her family for so many years. And then something else came into my head. I'd had my nan for nearly thirteen years, my whole life, ever since the day I was born. Jasmine had never had her at all.

The cemetery was almost empty, just two old ladies laying some flowers on a grave on the other side of the path. There was no sign of Kieran, but I was relieved he was okay and away from his dad. I couldn't wait to see him at school on Monday. Even though the nurse and Vivian had both said he was fine, I still needed to see him with my own eyes to believe it.

I picked up a small stone to place on his mum's grave, rubbing the dirt off until it was smooth and clean. As I got closer I could see there were some stones on there already, scattered across the grave. It was only when I kneeled down to place mine among them that I realized they were arranged in a particular way, to spell something. It was difficult to make out at first, especially close-up. I leaned back, my heart beginning to dance in my chest as the letters jumped out at me. Kieran had used lots of small stones to write:

25

Blind Panic!

I sprang up and looked around; scared Kieran might be watching me. Was he really at his aunt's like Vivian said? Or was he crouching down somewhere in the cemetery, waiting to see how I'd react? Gemma was always saying Kieran liked me, but surely this must be a joke. Or was that why he kept staring at me all the time? Why he'd hung around to watch me play rounders that day?

And then suddenly it hit me. The message was on his *mum's gravestone*. The M didn't stand for Maddie, it stood for Mum. I started to burn up, my cheeks red-hot. I felt so stupid for even thinking he'd left the message for me, that the M was for Maddie. He'd probably arranged the stones like that on the anniversary of the accident, a couple of days ago, just after he told me about his dad.

I ran out of the cemetery and all the way home, as if I could leave my embarrassment behind me. How could I be such an idiot? Just because I'd been thinking about Kieran non-stop since then, that didn't mean he'd given me a second thought. I ran faster and faster, desperate to get away, but it was still there, stuck inside my head – Kieran, the stones, the message, the whole stupid thing.

Mum and Charlie were in the lounge talking when I got back. The first thing I heard as I came through the front door was Jasmine's name. I hovered outside, listening, so churned up over everything and out of breath I could hardly think straight. Charlie was asking Mum what she was like. Asking her if she thought Jasmine was happy to have a new brother and when he could meet her – how he couldn't wait to tell her he'd been picked for the football team.

I stumbled back as if I'd been struck by a train. *Charlie in the football team?* And the first person he wanted to tell was *Jasmine*! She was going to take him away from me as well – my little brother who I'd looked after since the day he was born. He thought we were all going to play happy families. She'd be his new big sister. He didn't seem to have a clue that Jasmine was going to ruin everything, that our family would never be the same again.

I could still hear them talking but it was coming from far away, as if I'd left my body and floated up to the ceiling. I tried to calm down, to take a proper breath, but I couldn't do it, not without my ribbon. I raced upstairs to my room, reaching under my pillow, but it wasn't there. It was in my school bag. It had to be. I tore back downstairs, grabbed my bag and turned it upside down, spilling everything out on the floor – but I couldn't see it.

Mum came rushing out of the lounge. "What's going on?" she said, her face creased up with worry. "What's the matter?"

"I need my ribbon," I gasped. "I can't breathe. Where is it? I can't find it. I need it now!"

My skin was prickling all over like pins and needles but a million times worse. I lurched into the kitchen and started to open drawers, pulling things out, my breath coming faster and faster until the room began to spin.

"Stop it, Maddie! Calm down!" Mum came up behind me and tried to take hold of my arms but I pushed her off and ran back upstairs. There had to be an old bit of ribbon in my room somewhere, under the bed or at the back of my wardrobe. I was sure I'd seen one stuffed in there a few weeks ago when I was looking for my trainers…

Mum chased after me, catching me up as I flung the door open. "Stop it!" she said again, but louder. She grabbed hold of my arms, twisting me round to face her. "You don't need your ribbon. You just need to calm down. Look into my eyes, Maddie. Come on, breathe with me." She took a deep breath in through her nose.

I tried to focus on what she was saying. I forced myself to look at her and somehow managed to take a ragged breath. "Now breathe out," she said, blowing out of her mouth, and then she breathed in again. I breathed with her. In, out, in, out. My heart slowed down. The room stopped spinning. I collapsed against her, hot tears running down my face.

She held me tight, stroking my hair, whispering in my ear. "You're all right, Maddie. You just had a bit of a panic, that's all. I understand, sweetheart, it's a lot to get used to."

"What's the matter with me?" I sobbed. "Why can't I cope? Why do I need my stupid ribbon? Why can't I just be normal like everyone else?"

"You are normal; you're completely normal, you've just had a shock. It would be difficult for anyone to deal with what you're going through right now, but I'm here for you, Maddie, I'm going to look after you. You don't need a piece of ribbon to keep you safe any more."

She led me over to my bed and sat me down. I had no energy left to speak or even think, I just wanted to go to sleep. I crawled under my sheet and curled up in a ball. "I love you, Mum," I whispered as my eyes began to close. "I love you so, so much."

I slept all the way through until the morning, waking up groggy and confused. I glanced at my clock, blinking in surprise. It was half past nine. The longest sleep I'd had in months. The panic must've exhausted me. I lay in bed going over everything that had happened: fighting with Gemma, seeing the stones in the cemetery, overhearing Charlie talk about Jasmine, trying to find my ribbon. I curled up again, feeling wretched, wishing I was still asleep.

Mum knocked on my door just after ten and came in with orange juice and toast.

"Morning, sleepyhead," she said. "Nice to see you back in the world of the living!" She sat on my bed, holding out the juice while I pulled myself upright.

"Is Dad here?"

"Yep, he's downstairs making lunch. We're having a roast, one of his specials…"

"I suppose he'll be going off to see Jasmine later?" I said. I knew I sounded like a baby, I could almost taste the bitterness in my voice, but I couldn't help it.

"No, he's not seeing Jasmine today," said Mum. "She's up at the hospital. But they have had some better news. Apparently Sharon's responded really well to the latest treatment."

"I don't even know what's wrong with her," I said. I thought about her headscarf, how thin she was. "Has she got cancer?"

Mum nodded. "Yes she's got a rare type of leukaemia, cancer of the blood. She's been very ill."

I took a sip of drink, stalling. I didn't know what to say. I felt like the meanest person in the world for making such a fuss about everything, but I still didn't want Jasmine to be part of our family. Mum didn't say anything either; she didn't try to talk me round, but I could see from her face she was worried.

I stayed in my room all morning. Charlie came bursting in at one point. He wanted to tell me about getting picked for the team and talk about Jasmine, but I pulled my covers over my head and told him to leave me alone. He seemed to be so accepting of everything – Dad, Jasmine, our family changing – as if you could fix a family as easily as you could make a roast dinner.

It wasn't the most relaxing lunch. Mum and Dad were both trying way too hard and I found it difficult to even look at Dad, let alone talk to him. No one mentioned Jasmine but it felt as if she was in the kitchen with us anyway, taking up more space than all four of us put together. It was so tense I felt like screaming her name; just screaming it over and over and over to make everyone stop pretending.

As soon as we finished eating I went back up to my room and hid away for the rest of the day. It was obvious Mum and Charlie had made up their minds to welcome Jasmine into the family. I tried to imagine what it would be like – to spend time with her, to have an older sister. I even got my sketchbook out at one point and drew a picture of the whole family with Jasmine added in, but it looked all wrong.

However hard I tried to be positive, I couldn't get past the thought of her and Dad together.

Kieran was in the cemetery when I walked through on Monday morning. I started to grin as soon as I saw him. It was such a relief to know he was okay. "Hey, you're sitting on my bench!" I said as I came up the path.

"Oh it's your bench now, is it?" he shot back, moving up to make room for me. "That's funny. I didn't see your name on it anywhere."

"It's still mine," I said, laughing, "but I don't mind if you want to sit on it sometimes."

He looked different. Not his clothes, obviously, he was wearing his school uniform – it was more the way he was sitting there, with his shoulders down and his hands out of his pockets. As if he didn't expect the sky to fall in any more. Neither of us said anything for a minute and then we both started talking at the same time.

"Vivian said you were staying at…"

"I know you came to see me at the…"

"Go on, you first," I said.

He shrugged. "I was just going to say I know you came to see me at the hospital. I went for a check-up and one of the nurses told me. Well I'm assuming it was you. They said it was a pretty girl with dark hair and pale-blue eyes."

I started to burn up, remembering the stones on his mum's grave. Maybe the "M" did stand for Maddie after all.

"Are you okay?" I said to cover my embarrassment. "I mean the check-up. Was everything okay?"

He nodded, looking away. "It was only concussion. It happened that night, after I saw you here…on the anniversary." He took a stone out of his pocket, pressing it into the palm of his hand. "My dad was drunk and we got into a fight. He pushed me against the living room wall.

I don't think it was very hard but it's difficult to remember. They said I hit my head and blacked out. It wasn't really my dad's fault. He didn't mean to hurt me. I told them at the hospital but they still got social services involved and then the police."

I could feel tears stinging the corners of my eyes. He always tried to make it sound as if it was nothing, as if he didn't matter.

"What's going to happen now?"

He shrugged again, turning back to face me. "I'm staying with my aunt and uncle. It's okay, I suppose. Normal. I'll probably stay there right through the summer holidays until September. I've been seeing my dad but only when there's someone else there to supervise. He hasn't touched a drink since that night; at least that's what he says…"

I dug my nails into my palm. He'd been through so much. He'd lost his mum and now he'd lost his dad too.

"How about you, Maddie? Did you find out about your dad and the girl you saw by your locker?"

I nodded, feeling stupid suddenly; my problems were nothing compared to his. "Her name's Jasmine. She's my half-sister. My dad didn't know about her, so it's come out of the blue for him as well as for us."

I waited for him to say how lucky I was, or something like that, but he didn't say anything, he just reached across and took my hand, pressing the stone into my palm and then closing my fingers around it. A rush of butterflies filled my tummy. It was so unexpected I didn't know what to do.

"I'm supposed to be having a meeting with her today," I said, anxious to keep talking, to hide how shaky I was feeling, "in the Blue Room at nine. Vivian can't see us separately any more, it's a conflict of interests or something, so she wants us to go and talk to her together, but I'm not going. It's too weird. I don't even know her. How am I supposed to act like we're sisters when we're total strangers?"

I turned to look at him, to see what he was thinking, to see if he thought I was being stupid. Our faces were so close I had to shut my eyes for a second.

"Listen, Maddie, there's something I need to tell you."

I held my breath, wondering what it could be. I had no idea what he was going to say or how I'd react. It was like being right at the top of a roller coaster, in that split second before you go over the edge.

"The thing is," he said. "I can't tell you here, not in the cemetery. I'll meet you by your locker at nine, straight after my usual session with Vivian."

I let my breath out, half-relieved, half-disappointed. "Can't you tell me now?"

He shook his head. "I'll tell you later, I promise. We've got to go now anyway." He reached out for my hand again. I slipped the stone in my pocket and he pulled me up from the bench. "Come on, you don't want to be late…" He kept hold of my hand as we walked towards school.

Gemma was waiting for me at our usual place at the top of Banner Road. I told Kieran I'd see him later and ran towards her, desperate to sort things out. "I'm really sorry about Friday," I blurted out before she could say anything. "I didn't mean to snap at you. Please, *please* say we're still friends."

"Of course we're still friends," Gemma said. "It's me who should be saying sorry. I should've been more understanding. Just because *I'd* love to have a sister…" She trailed off, looking over my shoulder. "By the way, was that Kieran you were walking up the road with just now?"

I nodded, blushing, wondering if she'd noticed that we were holding hands. "I bumped into him in the cemetery. He's staying with his aunt and uncle."

"Did he tell you what happened? You know, that night?"

I nodded again but I didn't go into any details. "Listen,

I'm not seeing my counsellor any more so I can come straight to registration with you."

Mrs Palmer had lots of sheets of paper out on the tables so we could sign up for the summer fair. Gemma and I decided to run the art-and-crafts stall. We both loved art and it would be fun doing it together. I couldn't stop checking my watch. Kieran and Sally-Ann would be in the Blue Room with Vivian. I was dying to know what they were talking about, and what Kieran was going to say to me when we met up at nine.

I rushed to my locker as soon as registration finished. He didn't turn up straight away and I started to think he must've changed his mind. Vivian never ran over time. Jasmine would be waiting to go in – expecting me to show up for our meeting. I stood there for another minute or two and then made my way down the corridor to see if he was coming. The butterflies were back, but even worse, thinking about the way he'd held my hand all the way up Banner Road.

As I got closer to the Blue Room, I saw him up ahead, leaning against the wall. I stopped a few feet away. "I thought you told me to wait by my locker?"

"I know, but I decided it would be better if you came here instead. Less chance of you doing a runner."

"Doing a runner from what?" I said. But I knew. He

was talking about my meeting with Jasmine. He'd tricked me. "I thought you wanted to tell me something…"

"I do want to tell you something." He took a step closer. I held my breath, waiting. "It's easy to walk away when things get tough," he said, quoting Vivian word for word. "It's so much harder to stay."

"It's not the same," I said. But I knew it was. "It's too late anyway. The session's already started. I can't just barge in."

He looked at me, waiting. I closed my eyes. Kieran would never see his mum again. It was so difficult to get my head round that word "never". However angry he got, or however much he wanted it, it was *never* going to happen. She was gone *for ever*. I didn't want to push Dad away. I'd always miss my nan, but I still had both my parents. Gemma was right. I was lucky. But when I thought about sitting in the Blue Room with Jasmine…

"I'm scared," I whispered. "I'm scared of everything changing."

"You're not as scared as you think. You're the only person who's had the guts to stand up to me since my mum died…to come anywhere near me…"

He was making it sound as if I was strong and brave. He didn't realize how frightened I was inside. How my ribbon was in my bag. How I'd found it stuffed down the back of my bed and still needed it just to get through the day. How I'd never really done anything brave in my whole entire life.

His eyes never left my face. "If anyone can walk into that room, Maddie Wilkins – late, or early, or *anything* – it's you."

26
Being Brave

I stood outside the door for at least another five minutes, trying to work out a speech in my head, something to say as I walked in. I wanted to tell Jasmine that she would never be my sister, that I'd never forgive her for taking my dad away, but it was starting to feel so much more confusing than that. It's not as if it was her fault. It's not as if *any* of this was her fault.

I glanced back over my shoulder. Kieran was still there. He was still watching me. I wanted to be brave for him, to prove to him I could do it. I took a breath and grasped the doorknob. Just because I turned up to the meeting didn't mean I was welcoming Jasmine into my family. Dad might feel a bond with her, but she was still a stranger to me. I glanced back at Kieran one last time and then pushed the door open and walked in.

Vivian was sitting at the table by herself. I was so surprised I froze, worried that I'd got the wrong time, or misunderstood the whole arrangement.

"Hello, Maddie." She looked up, smiling. "I'm so pleased you're here. Come and sit down, it's just the two of us at the moment."

"Where's Jasmine?" I said. "I thought we were meeting together?"

"So did I," said Vivian, glancing up at the clock. "She said she was coming. Never mind. We'll make a start without her…"

"But I thought she'd be here. I was working out what to say. I was so scared and now she hasn't even bothered to turn up."

"Yes, it was very brave of you to come, Maddie."

I didn't feel brave. I was so nervous about seeing Jasmine I could barely think straight. I went over and sat in my chair. Vivian held the pad out to me but I shook my head.

"It was Kieran who persuaded me to come," I said. "I didn't want him to think I was a coward."

"Well there's not much chance of that, is there?" said Vivian, laughing.

"What do you mean? I'm scared of everything. He used to call me Maddie Mouse and he was right. That's what I've been like ever since my nan died – a frightened little mouse, too scared to face up to anything, too pathetic to get through the day without my purple ribbon!"

Vivian shook her head. She was about to say something but the door swung open and Jasmine walked in. She looked terrible. Her eyes were red and swollen and she was clutching a damp tissue in her hand.

"Hello, Jasmine," said Vivian. "I'm so pleased you're here."

"I'm sorry I'm late," she said. "I nearly bottled out, to be honest." She walked over to the table and sat down opposite me. I still couldn't get over how much she looked like Dad. Before Vivian could say anything, she went on, "I know you don't really want to see me, Maddie, your dad told me, he told me how upset you've been, and I swear I'll leave you alone after today, but there's something I need to tell you first."

I swallowed hard, my mouth dry. I didn't want to hear what she had to say. I didn't want to know how desperate she was. Why was Dad telling her stuff anyway?

She took a shaky breath, her eyes flickering across to Vivian and then back to me. "I never really wanted to meet my dad when I was growing up," she started. "I know it sounds weird, but my mum didn't talk about him much and we were happy. I did ask her about him a few times, especially as I got older, but it didn't exactly bother me, it wasn't like there was something missing, some big hole in my life. There was only one thing I wanted, one thing I couldn't have..." she paused, her eyes locking with mine, "and that was a sister."

She looked back down at her hands, shredding the tissue into tiny pieces. "I dreamed of having a sister, Maddie. I used to pretend sometimes. It sounds really lame, I know, but I had these two dolls, a big one and a little one, and I'd pretend one was me and one was my sister. I'd make up conversations about going shopping together and swapping clothes, stuff like that. Whenever Mum was working and I was at home by myself or with my childminder, I used to think how much more fun it would be if I had a sister. Someone to share things with..."

I thought about Gemma, how sad she was that her mum had lost the baby, how much she'd wanted a sister, how lucky I was to have Charlie.

Jasmine took another shaky breath, her eyes brimming with tears. She dabbed at them with her shredded tissue. "When my mum got ill she told me I was going to meet my dad and that he was going to help us. I flipped out, to tell you the truth. I didn't want to meet him; I was terrified – he was a total stranger as far as I was concerned. But then the first time we spoke on the phone he told me about you and Charlie."

She looked up at me, smiling through her tears.

"The minute I knew I had a sister I started to dream again. I couldn't wait to meet you, Maddie. I didn't want to mess up your family or anything; I just had this fantasy of what it would be like to have my own sister at last. I didn't stop to think how it would be for you, how freaked out you might be…" She stopped, shaking her head. "Anyway, I'm going on and on and I haven't given you a chance to say anything. But please don't hate me, Maddie, *please*. I'm not trying to take your place, I could never do that; I just wanted us to be friends…"

She trailed off, watching me, waiting to see what I'd say. I could feel this huge pressure like a giant boulder pressing down on my chest, squeezing the air out of my lungs. I didn't know what to do. I looked across the table at Vivian. Why didn't she help me? Why didn't she *say* something? The silence was so loud it was impossible to think, everything was so muddled up in my head. Jasmine was desperate to be my sister, but I didn't know how to let her in.

We were still sitting there when her phone rang

suddenly. "It's the hospital," she said, glancing at the screen. "I've got to go." She stood up grabbing her bag. "I really hope you believe me, Maddie, I meant every word…" She gave me one last pleading look and then turned and raced out of the room.

Vivian and I carried on sitting there for a bit. She probably thought I was horrible. She probably thought I was the biggest cow in the world for not giving Jasmine a chance. My stomach clenched up. I felt like I'd failed some massive test. I just wanted to crawl away and hide somewhere where no one could find me.

"I know you must think I'm the worst person," I said in the end. "Shall I just go now or what?"

"I wasn't thinking that at all," said Vivian. "I was actually thinking about something you said just before Jasmine came in. Something about how scared you are of everything. 'Too scared to face up to anything. Too pathetic to get through the day without my purple ribbon.' Do you remember?"

I nodded, wondering what she was getting at.

"You said you only came today because you didn't want Kieran to think you were a coward, and I said there's not much chance of that."

"I know, but—"

"But the thing is, Maddie, I'm beginning to think

289

you've invested this purple ribbon of yours with some kind of magic power."

"You don't understand," I said. "You don't know how frightened I am inside."

She tapped the table with her hand as if I'd proved her point. "Yes of course you are, but being frightened isn't the same as being a coward. The other day when I asked you who else knew about the girl in the cafe, you said, 'only Kieran, oh and Gemma, she's my best friend' – not just your friend, Maddie, your *best* friend – and yet when you first came to the nurture group, you didn't seem to be sure of your friendships at Church Vale at all. You said you didn't have any close friends…"

"Yes, but—"

"And then there's Kieran," she went on, interrupting me. "You cared about him enough to go up to the hospital. You told me you hate hospitals, that they remind you of Charlie being ill, and your nan, and yet you were brave enough to show him how much he mattered even though he did everything he could to push you away. *You* did that, Maddie, not your ribbon."

I shook my head, frowning. She was talking about me, but it didn't sound like me.

"And what about these sessions? You've never missed a single one. You've never refused to come, or run out in the middle. You've turned up and shared some of your deepest fears. And do you know something, Maddie? I've never even *seen* your purple ribbon."

My eyes filled with tears. I wanted to say it wasn't me, that I hadn't really done anything, that none of those things counted. But a tiny voice in my head was telling me that it was me, that they did count. I wasn't sure how, but somehow I'd managed to do all those things without my ribbon.

Vivian smiled at me across the table. "You're not a coward, Maddie. In fact, to tell you the truth, you're one of the bravest people I know."

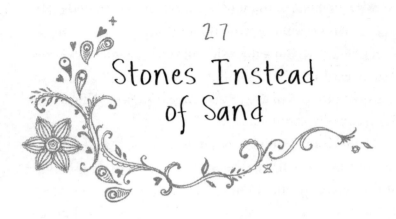

27
Stones Instead
of Sand

I rewrote my English homework that night, the one about a hole in our life. We'd already handed it in but I decided to do mine again even if Miss Owen refused to accept it. There was still a weird atmosphere at home; no one dared to mention Jasmine in front of me. When Mum came into my room to say goodnight, I almost asked her how you could hate someone but think you might really like them all at the same time.

Kieran was already in the cemetery when I got there the next morning. It was weird how normal it felt, as if we'd been meeting each other there for months. We walked up Banner Road together, talking about the meeting with Vivian and Jasmine. I told him how Jasmine said she'd always wanted a sister. How confusing it was.

"I saw her go in actually," he said. "She rushed past me as she came out of the toilets. I'll tell you something, she looked a lot more frightened than you."

"You're not taking her side, are you?" I said. "You know how scared I was!"

Kieran rolled his eyes. "Of course I'm not taking sides. It's not really about sides, is it?"

Gemma was waiting for me by the gates. She looked a bit embarrassed when she saw me coming up the road with Kieran. I think he must've realized. "See you later," he said, and melted into the crowds. I watched him go until I couldn't see him any more, my eyes fixed to the back of his head. The more time I spent with him, the more I wanted to be with him.

It was English straight after registration. I slipped into class a couple of minutes early to talk to Miss Owen. I explained about rewriting my homework and she said it was fine – that she'd stick it into my book and mark it straight away so she could hand it back with the others at the end of the lesson.

"I'm impressed, Maddie," she said. "I can't actually remember anyone *redoing* their work without being asked first."

Gemma arrived five minutes later. "Where did you go? I haven't told you about Nathan."

"What about him?"

"It's just, well, I don't think I like him any more."

"Gemma, what are you talking about? I thought you were crazy about him?"

She pulled a face. "I know, I was, I *am*, but he's never going to notice me, not in a million years. Not like you and Kieran. He's obviously mad about you."

I couldn't help grinning. "No he's not. Anyway, we're just friends."

"Do me a favour, Maddie. It couldn't be more obvious if you tried."

I was about to deny it again when Miss Owen cleared her throat and everyone stopped talking.

"Before we go on to the final chapters of *Holes*," she said. "I'm going to ask one or two of you to read out your homework from last week. There was such an amazing variety of ideas, and some of the pieces were extremely moving."

Her eyes began to scan the room. I automatically looked down. I was certain she wouldn't choose me anyway – I'd only just handed mine in – but a moment later she said, "Maddie. I'd like you to go first, please."

My head snapped up. It didn't mean I wanted to read

it out, just because I'd rewritten it. Why did she always pick on me? Why did she always choose *me* to get up in front of the class? Sweat dripped down my back. I glanced round at Kieran. Our eyes locked. He was giving me that look – the same look he'd given me yesterday just before I went into the meeting with Vivian and Jasmine. He thought I was brave. He thought I could do it.

I pushed my chair back and stood up slowly, making my way to the front of the room. Miss Owen handed me my book and I stood next to her desk, my mouth as dry as sand, convinced I wouldn't be able to make a sound. Never mind about *jumping* into a freezing cold swimming pool, this was like *diving* in head first.

"Just over seven months ago…" I started. My voice sounded terrible – squeaky and quiet like a mouse. I cleared my throat, swallowed hard and tried again. "Just over seven months ago my nan had a stroke and a week later she died. We were very close. She was more like a mum to me than a nan, and losing her left a massive hole in my life."

I peeked over the rim of my book. Everyone was watching me, waiting. I blinked hard and looked back down, blocking them out, forcing myself to keep speaking. "When I came back to school after the funeral, everything was different. I couldn't stop thinking about my nan, wishing she was still alive. I didn't really feel safe without her. I couldn't concentrate in class and my grades went down. I didn't know how to stop missing her so much."

My tongue was stuck to the roof of my mouth. I needed water. The first bit was hard enough to say, but the next bit was even harder. I gulped down my nerves and carried on. "Luckily I have two special friends at Church Vale who have helped me come to terms with losing my nan – who have helped me to see that I *am* strong enough to cope. First of all there's Gemma. She's funny and generous and kind and she accepts me for who I am. I can tell her anything, and I know she won't judge me or think less of me. I'm so lucky to have her as my best friend." I paused again, glancing up for a moment and then looking back to my book.

"My, um…second special friend is Kieran Black." A few people started murmuring, turning round to stare at Kieran at the back of the room. "Someone told me earlier today that I'm one of the bravest people they know. Maybe I did do something that was brave, but Kieran is so much braver than me. He's the bravest person I've ever met. The hole in his life can never be filled, but I really hope my friendship will help him as much as his friendship has helped me."

I lowered my book, staring down at my feet. I had no idea how Kieran would react, if he'd be angry with me for saying something so personal. There was a moment's silence and then he scraped back his chair and stood up. I held my breath, convinced he was going to walk out, that our friendship was over. But then the most extraordinary thing happened. He raised his hands and began to clap. For a second it was just him, but then Gemma joined in, and then Miss Owen, and a moment later the whole class was smiling and nodding and clapping as I made my way back to my place.

I don't think I stopped grinning for the rest of the lesson. It was like a miracle. I'd read my work out in front of the class without fainting or having a panic attack or running out. Nan would be so proud; I could almost hear her cheering, see her arms raised above her head. Miss Owen said she was giving me my first A for months and months. "What a brilliant way to end the year, Maddie," she said. "I knew you could do it."

Everyone was talking about it, saying they couldn't believe I'd written something so personal and especially about Kieran. I overheard someone say how surprised they were I'd had the guts to read it out and Gemma turned round and said, "Well if you think that was good, you should see her at rounders club – she's brilliant!"

"Come on then, *best friend*," she said, linking her arm through mine as we made our way out of English and down the corridor to maths. "You might want to warn me next time you're going to tell the entire class how kind and funny and generous I am!"

"What do you mean, *warn you*? I had no idea Miss Owen was going to ask me to read it out. I nearly died."

"I'm only joking," she said. "But, god, that stuff you said about Kieran and then the way he clapped. I had goosebumps all up my arms."

"It was all true," I said. "He has been a good friend and he's really helped me. So have you. I honestly meant every word."

I didn't see Kieran again for the rest of the day. He must have slipped out while Miss Owen was talking to me at the end of English. My tummy did a somersault every time I thought about what had happened. I'd basically told the entire class that he was one of my best friends.

He was still off school the next day. I was hoping he might be waiting for me in the cemetery but there was no sign of him. It was horrible; I didn't even have a number to text him. I went to see Vivian in the end, to tell her how worried I was. She did her best to reassure me. She said as far as she knew he was fine and that he'd be back at school by the end of the week.

"I heard about your English lesson," she said. "Mrs Palmer told me. I don't need to tell you how proud I am."

I smiled up at her, my face growing hot. "Thank you. And thank you for everything." I stood there for a moment, my arms hanging by my sides. I wanted to give her a hug, to show her how grateful I was, but I wasn't sure if it was the right thing to do. I don't think she had any idea how much she'd helped me.

"Um...do you think I'll be seeing you again?" I said in the end.

"I'm not sure," said Vivian. "There's only a week to go until the end of term, but if you and Jasmine want to come and see me together, one last time, I'm more than happy to arrange it with Mrs Palmer..."

Me and Jasmine. Together. *Again*.

"I'll think about it," I mumbled. "I'll let you know, okay?" I turned and raced off down the corridor. Me and Jasmine together. It still felt scary. But I couldn't help feeling a strange flutter of excitement at the same time.

It was the last rounders session after school. Gemma's last chance to impress Nathan. She was still insisting she didn't like him any more, but it was so obvious she did. I made her promise she'd wear her glasses just for this one game, just to prove to herself that she could actually hit the ball.

"It won't make any difference," she moaned as we trailed out of the changing rooms. "I'll still miss. I'm rubbish at rounders and that's all there is to it!"

Nathan was already on the field when we got there. We could see him standing by first base with Mr Skinner talking to someone. As we got closer I realized it was Kieran and that he was wearing his PE kit. I was so surprised I went running straight over to ask him what was going on.

"I've come to play rounders," he said, as if it was the most normal thing in the world – as if he hadn't been away for the past two days – as if the last time we saw each other I hadn't just told the entire class that he was one of my best friends.

"Kieran's joining us for the last session," said Mr Skinner. "Apparently he used to play in his primary school and he's keen to try out for the school team."

"I don't believe this," I said as we walked over to the others. "I thought you didn't *do* after-school clubs!"

"I didn't," he said. "But that was before you challenged me. And I'm on the other team, Maddie, so you'd better watch out!"

Kieran's team was batting first. It was weird playing

against him. I was dying to know what he thought about my essay and where he'd been for the past few days. I watched him as he got up to bat. He hadn't been with his aunt and uncle for very long but he'd changed so much. Almost as if they'd given him permission to enjoy himself again.

He was right about being good. He whacked the ball so far across the field he could have crawled round on his hands and knees and still scored a rounder. I could tell Mr Skinner was impressed and it was great to see him get a cheer from the rest of his team. I had to stop myself cheering along with them.

"Beat that, Maddie Wilkins!" he called out, running past me on third base.

"You just wait!" I yelled after him, although I didn't really care if I beat him or not, I was just happy he was there and that he was having a good time.

Gemma wasn't having such a good time. She missed at least three catches while we were fielding and when it was our turn to bat she refused point-blank to get up for her turn.

"There's no point," she wailed. "I'll never hit it and I'll just make an even bigger fool of myself than I already have."

"Come on, Gem, you have to. Just try to stay calm

and remember everything Charlie taught you."

"But I can't remember! That's the whole point – it was weeks ago!"

I pulled her up and gave her a quick hug. "Keep your glasses on and stay focused. You can do it, Gemma, I know you can!"

She stood with the bat in her hand, peering at the bowler. I half-closed my eyes, praying she'd hit the ball, even if she didn't score a rounder. A boy from our form called Hadif was bowling. He took a step forward, pulling his arm back at the same time. Gemma raised the bat ready. *Come on,* I whispered to myself. *Come on, come on.* Suddenly there was a crack, the sweetest sound in the world, and the ball was sailing over Hadif's head.

"Run!" screamed Nathan, and everyone started to chant, "Gem-ma, Gem-ma."

"I hit it!" she squealed, racing towards first base. "I hit the ball!"

She only got as far as second but it felt as if she'd scored the winning rounder.

Our side won 10–8 in the end. I scored two of the rounders and Mr Skinner said he definitely wanted me in the school team next year; my name was already on the list.

"I still hit the ball further than you did," said Kieran as

we made our way down Banner Road and into the cemetery. "So you didn't *officially* beat me."

"If it makes you feel better," I said, laughing. "I had no idea you were so competitive."

"There's lots you don't know about me," he said.

I glanced across at him. His face had clouded over, his shoulders hunched again. We stopped by the bench and sat down.

"My dad was in court yesterday; that's why I've been off school. I didn't have to go, but I wanted to."

"What happened?"

Kieran leaned back, sighing. "It's complicated. He's not going to prison, that's the main thing, but I won't be able to move back in with him. Not until he can show the courts he's stopped drinking. He has to sign up for this special treatment programme."

I turned to face him, drawing my knees up under my chin. "I don't think I've ever told you, but my mum works at this addiction clinic and I'm pretty sure your dad goes there, or used to go there. She doesn't talk about it or anything, it's completely confidential, but I just wanted you to know."

"It's all right," he said. "I already knew."

We sat in silence for a bit. He took a stone out of his pocket. It was small and round and very smooth. "We went to Brighton once," he said rubbing the stone around in his hand. "I was only about five. I was so excited on the drive down, it was my first trip to the seaside, but when we arrived and I realized it was a stony beach, that there was no sand, I couldn't stop crying. I was devastated. I wanted to make sandcastles with my dad, proper ones with moats and tunnels; I'd been planning it all the way there."

He stared ahead as if he was remembering the actual day, as if he was still five years old.

"I was in such a state, my mum sat me on her lap and she told me a story about the stones. She said there once lived a prince who was allergic to sand. He loved the seaside, but whenever his skin came into contact with sand he came out in blisters. The prince lived right by a beautiful beach, but year after year he had to stay inside the palace while all the other children played on the sand and swam in the sea.

"The Queen couldn't bear to see her son so upset so one summer she arranged for a massive delivery of stones – hundreds and thousands and millions of them to be delivered to the beach and laid on top of the sand. She told the little boy that stones were better than sand – that they didn't get stuck in-between your toes or ruin your picnic. And so that year, for the first time ever, the Prince was able to play on the beach like everyone else."

He turned to face me, his eyes bright with tears. "She had lots of stories," he said. "But the one about the stones is my favourite."

"It's a beautiful story," I said, blinking back tears myself. "It reminds me of my nan. She used to say there's only one side of life worth looking on, and that's the bright side."

"In other words, stones can be just as good as sand."

"Exactly," I said, smiling. "And sometimes they might even be better."

28

Pancakes for Tea

Dad and I had a long talk on Sunday morning. I told him about the note Sharon left on Nan's grave and he explained what happened, how Sharon had written to Nan after she was first diagnosed with cancer to tell her about Jasmine. How she wanted Jasmine to meet her family and thought contacting Nan first would be the best way to go about it.

"Apparently Nan was thrilled. She called Sharon straight away and they made arrangements to meet up, but Sharon lost her nerve and backed out at the last minute. Nan didn't say a word to me or Mum about it, but she told her friend Bessie and it was Bessie who contacted

Sharon to let her know Nan had passed away."

"It must've been a terrible shock," I said.

"It was a *massive* shock. That's when Sharon decided she had to let Jasmine meet the rest of her family. You can't imagine how guilty she feels that Jasmine and Nan never got to meet. That's why she left that note saying sorry. She was so worried about her own diagnosis; it never occurred to her that Nan might fall ill and die before her."

"What was it like when you first met Jasmine?" I said, half-wanting to know, half-dreading it. It was the one thing I'd been too scared to ask up until now. "How long was it after you first met up with Sharon?"

"I called Jasmine a few days later and we had a long chat on the phone, but the first time we actually met was the day we got back from the lake. It wasn't planned or anything, but do you remember the phone rang in the car? Well the hospital had called to say Sharon had taken a turn for the worse and Jasmine couldn't get hold of the friend she was staying with and she didn't know who else to call..."

"But it was *Sharon* who rang you that day," I said, confused. "I saw her name come up on your phone..."

"That was only because Jasmine had Sharon's phone. It was Jasmine who actually called."

"And what was it like, then, the moment you met her? How did you feel?"

Dad smiled. "Nervous. Scared. Curious. Guilty. A whole mix of emotions. It was frantic at the hospital, and then later on when we finally got the chance to chat I ended up talking about you and Charlie for most of the time, telling her how wonderful you both are..." He trailed off, glancing down at his watch. "Listen, I'm sorry, love, but I've got to pop up to the hospital now..."

I wanted to carry on talking. There was so much I needed to know, like how often he'd be seeing Jasmine, and if he'd be bringing her over to ours, and if he loved her as much as he loved me and Charlie. I still found it difficult to imagine them spending time together.

"We'll talk more later," said Dad, reaching for his keys. "I'll be home in time for lunch. Mum's making a roast so she might need some help."

I pulled a face. *Mum? Making a roast?*

"Don't say it like that, Mads," he laughed. "There's a first time for everything!"

I opened my mouth and then closed it again. I was doing what I always do – expecting everything to be a certain way – *the same way.*

"Do you promise you'll be back?" I said, trying not to feel jealous.

"Promise," he said. "Cross my heart."

Mum called me down at twelve to lay the table. I'd just about finished, and everything was ready, when Dad rung to say he was going to be late. I heard Mum say there was no hurry; it would give her a chance to put her feet up. But then he rang again at two and again at three and by that time the lunch was ruined and Charlie was out in the garden kicking a ball against the wall.

"I knew this would happen," I said to Mum. She'd taken the roasting dish out of the oven and was trying to pick all the burned bits off from around the edges. "It was so obvious. I knew he wouldn't be back in time…"

"You know what it's like in hospital, Mads. Everything takes for ever. A doctor says he'll come round to see you and you can still be waiting two hours later."

"Yes, but why is that more important to Dad than being here with us? Why is he putting Sharon and Jasmine first?"

Mum stopped picking off the burned bits and looked up. "Maddie, my love, I know it's difficult but you've got to be really grown-up about this, we all have. Sharon is very ill and the simple fact is Jasmine needs Dad more than we do at the moment."

It was so frustrating, so difficult to express how messed up my feelings were. "I know you're right, and I *am* trying.

But I honestly don't know how to stop feeling so jealous…"

Mum nodded at me, smiling. "Now that's a feeling I *do* understand."

"What do you mean? Do you feel jealous of Jasmine too?"

"Well not so much now I've actually *met* her, but seriously, Mads, those first few weeks when Dad was seeing Sharon and then getting to know Jasmine, my head was all over the place. Why do you think I ran away to Aunty Hat for the weekend? An ex-girlfriend *and* a new daughter – you'd have to be made of steel not to feel jealous in that situation!"

"I had no idea. I thought you just wanted to get away."

"And talking of feeling jealous, Mads," said Mum quietly. "There's something else I've never told you." She gave a little laugh, as if she was embarrassed. "I know it sounds ridiculous, a grown woman like me, but sometimes I used to be jealous of you and your nan."

"Jealous of me and Nan? What do you mean?"

"Well, when you were a little girl, after Charlie was born and Nan moved in to help out, if you ever fell over, or had a bad dream, it was always your nan you cried for. She was the only one you wanted. We'd been so close before, me and you, but everything changed. The two of you were always giggling, your heads together, like you were sharing a secret joke. I remember once you were laughing about something and even when you told me what it was, I still didn't get it, and that just made you laugh even more."

I stared at her, amazed. I couldn't believe it. Mum had been jealous of me and Nan.

She pushed the roasting tin towards me. "Hey, fancy some burned potato with crispy carrots?" she said, smiling again. "It tastes a whole lot better than it looks!"

We stood there picking at the food together, talking. I hadn't really thought about how difficult it must be for Mum, how she was sharing Dad too, or how difficult it must've been when Charlie was little and Nan was living with us. It was probably the first time she'd ever opened up to me about her feelings, almost as if she was seeing me in a different way. "This is nice," I said shyly, enjoying how close I felt to her.

"Really nice," said Mum nodding. "I'll have to make sure I burn the dinner more often!"

The next few hours seemed to crawl by in slow motion. Charlie came in from the garden and we all sat there waiting for the phone to ring. I knew Mum was right, that Dad wasn't up at the hospital because he loved Jasmine more than he loved us, but it didn't make it any easier.

He finally called again at half past four. Mum spoke for a bit and then turned to face us.

"They're ready to leave the hospital," she explained, "but the friend who's been looking after Jasmine is out for the evening and Dad doesn't want to leave Jasmine on her own."

"Tell him to bring her here then," Charlie said straight away.

Mum looked across at me. My stomach clenched up.

"Come on, Maddie," said Charlie. "I've been dying to meet her ever since we found out!"

I wanted to say no, I wanted to run a million miles away, but I nodded slowly, forcing a smile onto my face. "Okay," I said. "I don't mind."

"Why don't you bring her round here?" Mum said into the phone. Her eyes never left my face for a second. When she'd finished talking she came over and put her arms round me. "You've made me so, so proud," she said. "And you, Charlie. I think you're both fantastic."

Charlie started to rush around like an idiot. "I need to tidy my room and we should make a welcome banner or something…"

"Calm down," said Mum, laughing. "She's only coming in for a cup of tea and something to eat."

They arrived about half an hour later. I was so nervous

I could barely breathe. Jasmine hung back behind Dad, looking just as scared as I was feeling. The last time we'd seen each other had been in the Blue Room with Vivian. Mum ushered them in and then went into the kitchen to put the kettle on. Sharon was much better apparently; they'd just had to wait ages for some test results before they left.

"You must be starving," said Mum, bringing in a pot of tea with a plate of biscuits. "The lunch got burned to a crisp, I'm afraid."

"We could always have pancakes," said Charlie, blushing bright red. He hadn't actually said a thing since Jasmine arrived. I think it was the first time I'd ever seen him lost for words.

"Don't be stupid," I said. "We never have pancakes for tea."

"But we could," he insisted. "It's not like there's a rule that says you can't have pancakes for tea, just because we usually have them for breakfast."

There is a rule, I thought. *There are rules for everything, but no one seems to follow them any more.*

"Oh I love pancakes," said Jasmine. "I'll help make them – if you like?"

Mum, Dad and Charlie all turned to look at me, waiting for me to say it was okay. As if they were frightened

I might collapse in a heap if we did things differently for once. I didn't want to be the one to spoil things, however anxious I was feeling; I mean, it was only pancakes.

"Come on then," I said sticking my chin out. "Who says we can't have pancakes for tea!"

The pancakes were a huge success. Mum made the mixture and then me, Charlie and Jasmine took turns cooking them. We made a massive pile and put every kind of topping on the table that we could think of: lemon, sugar, jam, peanut butter, cream cheese and chocolate spread. Mum even dug out some old hundreds and thousands from the cupboard to sprinkle on top.

Later on, when we'd finished eating and clearing up, Jasmine said she had some presents for us. She'd bought them ages ago; as soon as she found out she had a new brother and sister. She'd made Dad stop at her flat on the way back from the hospital so she could bring them over and give them to us this evening.

She took Charlie's out first. It was a brand-new football and she said she couldn't wait to see him play in one of his school matches. Charlie had gone all shy again, blushing and saying thank you about a hundred times before he raced into the garden to try it out.

Jasmine handed me mine next. It was wrapped in purple paper with a purple satin ribbon.

"I hope you like it," she said. "Your dad told me how much you love purple wrapping paper and ribbon so I've got that right at least."

It was a beautiful, blank book with *A Place to Doodle and Sketch* written across the front. Just the sort of thing I love. It reminded me of Vivian's sessions and the bright-yellow pad I'd been doodling on for the past four weeks. She'd be amazed if she could see me and Jasmine sitting in the same room together.

"Thank you," I said, sounding just as shy as Charlie. "This is great, I love drawing. Um…I've got something for you too."

I ran upstairs, grabbed the photo of Nan off my bedside table, the one of her blowing out her birthday candles, and ran back down again.

"This was our nan," I said handing it to Jasmine. "I'd like you to have it. I really wish you'd had the chance to meet her. She was so special."

Jasmine stayed quite late. Dad dropped her back at her flat just before ten. She told us all about her mum, and moving, and how hard she'd found it to settle into Church Vale. She said she'd started to make friends but it wasn't easy. Mum was right, and Gemma, she seemed really nice, but I still got a funny feeling in my tummy when she left with Dad.

"You did so well," said Mum when she came in to say goodnight. I'd been sketching in my new book. A picture of a beach covered in stones, just like the beach in Kieran's story. "I know I said it before but I'm so proud of you, Maddie. I could see how hard it was for you, but you really made Jasmine feel welcome…"

I was proud as well. And a little bit excited. I liked Jasmine. I still couldn't believe we were related, but it was obvious she felt lucky to have me and Charlie in her life and I think, deep down, I knew that we were lucky too. When I finished my sketch I tore it out and wrote a message on the back. It was for Vivian – to say thank you.

It was only later when I turned the light out and snuggled down to go to sleep that I realized I hadn't checked to see if my purple ribbon was under my pillow. And then I realized something else – that when I'd unwrapped Jasmine's present earlier, I'd scrunched up the paper *and* the ribbon, without giving it a second thought, and chucked the whole lot in the bin.

Vivian was right. I'd given my purple ribbon all sorts of magic powers, but I didn't need it any more. I had my friends and my family and a new sister. I ran my hand over my tummy. No knot of anxiety, just an excited flutter at the thought of telling Gemma about my evening with Jasmine, and seeing Kieran on the way to school.

Nan was right too. It was so sad she never got to meet Jasmine – that she wasn't here to welcome her into the family. But I know exactly what she'd say if she was. I could almost hear her saying it – looking down from heaven with a big jammy doughnut in her hand.

Sometimes, Maddie Wilkins, the scariest things really do turn out to be the best.

Also by Anne-Marie Conway

Butterfly Summer

In her summer of secrets, all Becky knows
is that everything can change in the beat of
a butterfly's wing...

When Becky finds an old photo in a box under her
mum's bed, everything she thought she knew comes
crashing down. The only place she finds comfort is at the
Butterfly Garden with her new friend, Rosa May. But with
her wild ways, and unpredictable temper, is Rosa May
hiding something as well? In the heat of the sun-drenched
summer, it seems that Becky is the only one in the dark...

Mesmerizing and mysterious, Butterfly Summer *is a haunting
tale of intense friendship and dangerous discovery.*

ISBN: 9781409538592
EPUB: 9781409541738   KINDLE: 9781409541745

The unforgettable story of a new friendship,
a terrible tragedy and a long-buried lie.
Winner of the Southwark Book Award 2014

When Lizzie and Bee meet on holiday, it feels as if they
were always meant to be friends. Escaping their parents and
exploring, everything seems perfect in the hot summer sun.
But as the two girls grow closer, strange questions rise to
the surface... Is Lizzie really an only child? Why has Bee's
dad disappeared? And why, as the holiday comes to an end,
are the two girls forbidden from seeing each other again?

Could one dark secret from the past hold the answer?
Could one fateful night keep Lizzie and Bee apart...for ever?

ISBN: 9781409561903
EPUB: 9781409562665   KINDLE: 9781409561909

Acknowledgements

I would like to say a big thank you to Phaedra for her help and advice when I started planning *Tangled Secrets*. And to Paula and Andreas for their ongoing help and support througout the writing process.